THE ALPHA PLAGUE - BOOK 2

A POST-APOCALYPTIC ACTION THRILLER

MICHAEL ROBERTSON

Email: subscribers@michaelrobertson.co.uk

Edited by:

Terri King - http://terri-king.wix.com/editing
And
Pauline Nolet - http://www.paulinenolet.com

Cover Design by Dusty Crosley

The Alpha Plague 2

Michael Robertson
© 2015 Michael Robertson

The Alpha Plague 2 is a work of fiction. The characters, incidents, situations, and all dialogue are entirely a product of the author's imagination, or are used fictitiously and are not in any way representative of real people, places or things.

Any resemblance to persons living or dead is entirely coincidental.

MAILING LIST

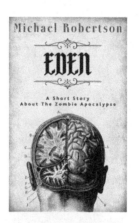

Michael Robertson

EDEN

**A Short Story
About The Zombie Apocalypse**

RAT RUN

A POST-APOCALYPTIC TALE

Michael Robertson

CHAPTER 1

Rhys walked down the centre of the lowered drawbridge and squinted against the setting sun. The city would be incinerated in just five hours' time. Anxiety knotted in his stomach and his legs ached. Hopefully he had long enough to get to The Alpha Tower in the middle of the city and back again.

Five hours seemed like a long time, but with scores of diseased and bloodthirsty lunatics to get through, it felt like nowhere near long enough. What had appeared to be a good idea ten minutes ago suddenly looked a lot worse when faced with the stark reality of it. He could have told Flynn that Mummy died, but he would have to carry the guilt that went with that for the rest of his days.

Each step forward weighed heavy with reluctance, and Rhys struggled to lift his feet. His shoes scraped the ground as he trudged along. Grief tightened his chest and burned his throat. He stared straight ahead at the city's skyline. If he looked behind, he'd see Flynn as he watched him from the backseat of the squad car. He'd see Vicky in the bridge's control booth. The sight of his son's face would make him go back in a heartbeat. The prospect of escape with Vicky would make it too hard to continue.

Remorse sat as a damp weight in his chest and uncertainty nestled in his gut, heavy and impossible to digest. Vicky wasn't a stranger but as good as. He'd placed a lot of trust in someone he'd only known for a day.

He pushed forward.

A strong wind howled across the open space and blasted into his right side. The undulating gusts were the only sounds he could hear in the otherwise desolate environment. The stillness didn't fool Rhys though; chaos lurked beneath it.

Rhys continued to scan the city in front of him. The open space that separated the bridge and the first line of towers seemed empty. The thin alleyways between the tall buildings were dark and quiet, and the only sign of movement was a sheet of yellowing newspaper that drifted along the deserted street.

A glance up at the incomplete towers on his left and a chill ran through Rhys. Fatigue already gripped his body, but when he relived the chase up those damn buildings… God knows how he found the strength to outrun those things to the top. God knows where he would find the strength should he need it again.

While he continued to scan around, Rhys moved from the middle of the bridge over to the right side. He looked down to where he and Vicky had dragged the boat into the water. The muddy riverbank had been churned up like a battlefield from the sheer amount of diseased that had chased them down there. It may have been quiet at that moment, but the memory of their ravenous screams roared through Rhys' mind.

The boat they'd used to get across the river remained teth-ered on the other side. Not that anyone would want to use it to get back into Summit City, but they should have capsized the thing so no one could even entertain the idea.

Another look down at the water and Rhys stopped dead. His breath left him in an involuntary gasp.

The sun may have been lower in the sky than before, but it still provided enough light for Rhys to see through the shallow water. A mixture of colours sat just beneath the surface. About ten metres in, the technicolour swathe vanished. Maybe the water got too deep to see any more than that. Maybe the diseased recognised when they'd been beaten and gave up in their attempt to catch the boat.

The colours were tinted through a rose lens of diluted blood, although the tint wasn't dark enough to hide what Rhys saw. A dry gulp did nothing to relieve his throat as he looked at the hundreds of diseased, all drowned as they lay beneath the surface.

None of them moved but their stillness didn't fool Rhys. They could come alive at any moment, desperate to pull on any kicking legs, and chow down. Vicky had said they drowned in water, but Rhys wouldn't be the one to test if they were dead or not.

Their earlier escape replayed in his mind. He saw the diseased as they fell to his baseball bat and sank beneath the water's surface. He saw their bloody maws spread wide as they thrashed, kicked, and writhed in panic. Yet, even as they drowned, they still bit at the air between them. Not even their impending end could temper their desire to get at Vicky and him. A cold chill snapped through him when he saw their bloody eyes in his mind.

A shake of his head and Rhys moved away from the right side of the bridge and crossed over to the left.

As he walked, he screwed his nose up when the fetid reek of death ran up it. A look down at his feet and he saw the sludgy, bloody secretion left behind by the diseased who'd been barricaded by the police. They may be long gone, but their stench hung heavy in the air. A small amount of bile lifted into Rhys' throat. He swallowed, but it did nothing to relieve the sharp acidic burn.

When a strong breeze blew across his face, it banished the smell momentarily. Before long, it returned with force, its vinegary kick so aggressive, he flinched.

Once on the left side of the bridge, Rhys looked down. Boats lined the shoreline all the way along; mostly rowboats, but a few speedboats and other smaller vessels bobbed in the water. If only they'd picked that side to escape from earlier... He shook his head to himself. All that struggle for nothing.

At the end of the bridge, closer to the half-built towers, the food pods waited; the trapped woman must still be inside one of them. Another check to the open space beyond the pods. The vast area was easily as big as six football fields and littered with the evidence of carnage, but still no sight of the diseased—long may it stay that way. Rhys looked at the food pods again. Like before, they seemed like the best place to hide.

Rhys scooted over to one of the pods, pressed his back into the sun-heated shutters that encased it, and dropped down into a crouch.

For the first time since he'd stepped onto the bridge, he looked back across the river. From his current position, he couldn't see his boy but he saw Vicky. He gave her a thumbs up, which she returned.

A loud *thunk* snapped through the near silence. Seconds later, the heavy groan of the bridge's motor yawned to life. Rhys watched as the bridge split in two. Both sides rose and pulled away from one another in a lethargic stretch.

The higher the bridge lifted, the harder Rhys' heart thudded. He'd made his choice; hopefully, he'd made the right one.

A diseased scream filled the air. It ran goose bumps up Rhys' arms and down the back of his neck. The sound of the bridge had clearly drawn them out, but when he looked around, he saw nothing… nothing yet, at least.

Having initially chosen the closest pod to hide by, Rhys moved down a couple more. If the diseased descended upon the bridge—which is exactly what they should do if they could be judged by their previous behaviour—then he needed to be farther away. He stopped in front of the one he'd hidden by earlier, the one with the woman inside.

The slight coolness of late afternoon may have lowered the temperature by a degree or two, but when he pressed his face against the steel shutter to listen out for the woman within the pod, the hot metal stung his ear. He heard nothing. *Damn! Maybe she'd killed herself.*

When another diseased scream called out, louder and closer than the one before, Rhys pulled his face away and drew a sharp intake of breath. He watched the bridge rise and waited for them to appear as his pulse ratcheted up a notch.

A deep breath in through his nose and a slow release through his mouth, and Rhys focused on trying to calm down. He repeated the process, his eyes wide as he looked out for the first signs of trouble.

Rhys moved across the front of the pod and slid down the side farthest away from the bridge. He had to assume they'd all head straight for the noise. If they did, he'd just made himself much harder to see. If they didn't… well, he couldn't plan for that.

A loud bang on the other side of the shutter caused Rhys' heart to jump and it damn near lodged in his throat. *Fuck!* The woman inside obviously hadn't offed herself. Earlier that day, her cries had been lost to the noise of the diseased. In the relative quiet, she sounded much louder than before. If she gave the game away…

Another loud bang and Rhys pushed his face into one of the small gaps between the metal shutters. The hot steel stung each cheek as he hissed, "Shut up."

When he pulled back, a wide and feral eyeball appeared at the gap. The shadows hid the rest of the person behind it and made the lone organ look like something from a horror film. The woman's voice came out in a wavered whimper. "Help me, please."

"Shut up and I might," Rhys said.

"But you'll leave me like you did last time."

Rhys lost his words. She recognised him?

"Help!"

"*Shut up*," Rhys said through gritted teeth. "I'll get you out of there, but you need to listen to me."

The woman in the booth sighed but didn't reply.

The steel shutters surrounded the food pods in their entirety. Unlike the shops in the city, they didn't have card readers on the outside. "I'm going to The Alpha Tower to release the shutters. The entire city's locked down in exactly the same way as this pod is. There are thousands of people trapped at the moment. I have to activate the central control to free everyone."

"Why's everything locked down?" the woman asked.

"There's a disease ravaging the city."

"What the fuck?"

"It's like a zombie virus."

"*Zombies*?"

"I know," Rhys said. "It sounds far-fetched, right? I wouldn't believe it either. Some kind of virus has broken out and has infected hundreds of people in Summit City. In effect, it's turned them into zombies; except not the slow, shuffling types. These fuckers move like steam trains and they want nothing more than to sink their teeth square into your face."

The woman didn't reply—Rhys wouldn't have in her situation either. His most likely response would have been 'get ta fuck'. Not that he had any Scottish in him; he just liked to use the phrase.

"The shutters are a defence against them," he explained. "The people who designed this city had quarantining in mind. Looks like we're the lucky ones to be here when the need arose."

Another diseased scream—even closer—and Rhys lowered his tone. "Anyway, what I need to do is get to The Alpha Tower, deactivate the city defence system so all the shutters lift up, and then everyone can escape. It may not have felt like it over these past few hours, but you're in a great position. The only way to survive is to get out of this city, and fast. There are boats down on the river in front of you. If you get in one of them, you'll be able to get to the other side and be free. The diseased can't swim."

The wide eye continued to stare at him.

"Look, you may think I'm nuts, but all I'm going to say is get out of here the second you can. If you hang around too long, you're fucked. Also, bear in mind that most people will be infected. If you're unsure, take out whoever's running at you. You can kill them if you lead them to water and go across; they'll drown trying to follow you. Another way is to deliver a serious brain trauma—body shots won't cut it."

Yet another scream and Rhys lowered his voice more, "Look, I've got to go." When he heard the woman inhale as if to speak, he cut her off. "If you keep quiet, I can get away from here. I'm your only hope. Please, trust me; I'll do *everything* in my power to get the shutters lifted. If you shout your mouth off now, we're both fucked." He looked at Flynn's Superman watch. "In five hours' time the entire city will be incinerated. I need every spare minute to help free as many of you as possible."

The eye widened more and then moved up and down in a nod.

Rhys pulled away from her and walked around the pod. It took him even farther away from the bridge and closer to the open space between him and the sky-scraping hell on the other side.

When he looked across at where he had to run to, he finally saw the chaos as it spilled out of the city. Each alleyway vomited lines of diseased. They flooded out at a sprint and lit up the air with shrill cries.

The pod threw a deep shadow, which he stayed hidden in as the diseased headed for the drawbridge. They ran with their stumbling gait, faster than most humans, but uncoordinated as fuck. They always seemed on the very limit of their balance.

At some point, the flow of diseased would stop. It had to. Then he'd make his move.

When he saw the man, Rhys' breath caught in his throat. The guy obviously wasn't infected; he stood in the doorway of one of the tower blocks, clutching some kind of weapon, an axe maybe. With it raised and ready to use, he had his back pressed into a wall as the stream of diseased rushed past. They ran towards the noise of the drawbridge with a single-minded focus; the sound seemed to provide a loud enough distraction to allow the man to remain hidden. Lucky for him that Rhys had chosen to re-enter the city at that point. If one of those bastards saw him, insanity would rain down on the poor guy.

With his attention divided between the man in the

doorway and the stream of clumsy diseased headed for the bridge, Rhys relaxed slightly. The diseased didn't notice the man and the man kept himself safe and out of the way. At least he seemed to know how to remain hidden.

AFTER A FEW MINUTES, THE SOUND OF THE DRAWBRIDGE DIED down and the diseased stragglers stumbled across the open space towards it. A scan of the opposite side, and Rhys saw what appeared to be the last few as they ran up the alleyway closest to the man. If only Rhys could tell the man opposite that he just had a few more diseased to hide away from.

The man then moved.

"Stay there," Rhys muttered. If the guy had a little more patience, he'd be fine. With the urge to shout across the open space balled in his throat, Rhys grimaced and watched on.

The three diseased rushed up the alleyway next to the man as the man continued to emerge from his hiding place.

The very second the man stepped out, the diseased appeared next to him. Both the man and the three diseased halted in their tracks and stared at one another.

When the lead diseased screamed, time stopped for Rhys. The other two joined the chorus. If they made much more noise, it would attract the horde by the bridge. If the horde joined the fight, Rhys had no chance of getting into the city.

The man's stupidity had suddenly become his problem.

CHAPTER 2

R hys looked at the man with the three diseased around him and then to the raised drawbridge. It may not have lifted fully, but it had lifted enough to create an effective barrier against the diseased. As one, they stood before the rising roadway and screamed and roared. Some punched it as if their fury had to be released. With no way to get across the river to Flynn and Vicky, but occupied by their pointless quest anyway, the mindless mob were in the perfect place to give Rhys an opportunity to slip into the city.

First, however, he had to cross the open space to get there... and do something to help the man.

The distance Rhys had to travel may have been over two hundred metres, but it didn't prevent him from seeing the man's size. Both broad and tall, he looked as well built to survive as anyone and had a good few inches on even the tallest of the three diseased. However, his size meant jack shit if the others at the bridge saw him. The Hulk would have a hard time against that crowd.

The walkie-talkie shook in Rhys' trembling hand when he pulled it from his pocket. Two large dials sat prominently on its front, one for the channels and one for the volume. A check across the river and he saw Vicky in the control booth, the London skyline prominent behind her. He switched the walkie-talkie on and pressed the button on the side. "Vicky, it's Rhys; if you can hear me, give me a thumbs up."

Rhys could only see Vicky as a silhouette through the booth's cloudy glass windows, so he couldn't tell if she'd heard him or not. A few seconds later, she stuck her arm out of the side and gave him a thumbs up.

"Good," Rhys said. "Don't say anything; otherwise, your voice will lead them straight to me. I have a problem. Some idiot was hiding in the entranceway to one of the buildings and is now fighting three diseased. If the others see what's going on, they'll lynch him and I won't stand a chance of getting into the city. I need you to distract them while I go and help him out."

Rhys watched the booth and nothing happened. Of course nothing happened; he'd hardly given her a plan of action, just a big fucking problem.

Then she stepped out of the booth and walked off. Because of the raised drawbridge, she disappeared from sight almost immediately. As Rhys stood there, he chewed on his bottom lip. Adrenaline pulsed through his veins and he shook worse than before.

A loud continuous beep then sounded out on the other side of the river. The diseased close to the raised bridge lifted their heads like a pack of dogs in response to a whistle. Rhys couldn't help but smile at Vicky's ingenuity. "Good girl."

The frenzy that had gripped the group only moments before ratcheted up. The diseased hurled themselves at the raised asphalt, and the roars turned to bellows. The screams rang so shrill they hit a pitch that sounded like it could break glass. Bloody maws snapped and they pushed one another aside to launch themselves at the bridge as if repeated attempts would make the immoveable barrier yield.

Rhys jumped when he looked down to see the eyeball in the booth. It still watched him through the gap in the shutters. He leaned close, careful to keep his face from the hot steel this time, and whispered, "Look, I'm sorry I told you to shut up. I understand you're scared in there. I would be too, but don't worry, everything's going to be okay. I'm going to get to The Alpha Tower and get these damn shutters up. Just be ready for it when it happens, okay?"

A quiet voice answered, "Okay."

"What's your name, love?"

"Adele."

"Okay, Adele, I promise I'll do everything to make sure the shutters are raised. When they are, get across the river. Don't hang about, okay?"

"Okay."

After a deep breath, Rhys watched as the man defended himself against the three diseased. He checked his watch to see he had less than five hours already. A sharp nod at the woman in the booth and he said, "Okay."

CHAPTER 3

Rhys' legs burned as much as before, if not more. Each time one of his feet hit the ground, he stumbled. Without a proper rest since everything kicked off, his body felt like it could give up on him at any moment.

As he ran—the walkie-talkie in one trouser pocket, the lump of wood in the other—he listened to the prolonged car horn; much longer and she'd kill the battery. A glance at the drawbridge and he saw the creatures as furious as ever, their full attention still directed at the immoveable barrier that kept them contained. As long as they stayed there, he could help the man with the axe fight off the diseased.

Rhys looked left at the two incomplete towers and the florist's. The flower shop door remained open, the vibrancy of the stock dulled by huge swathes of red. The memory of when he found the dead woman ran a shock through his heart. Thank god none of that blood had belonged to Vicky. If only he had her by his side now.

Now that he'd gotten closer, Rhys guessed the man was at least six feet and four inches. Broad shouldered and with thick arms, he stood in front of Building Thirteen and fended the diseased off with the handle of his axe. Like a piston, he punched sharp jabs at the creatures, driving back the closest one each time with a heavy blow.

The same pattern repeated after each hit; the monsters stumbled back, shook their heads as if to discard their dizziness, and approached the guy again with renewed vigour. The man showed no signs of fatigue, either. He looked like he could go all day if he needed to. His weapon remained his biggest handicap; if he buried the axe blade into the skull of one of the monsters, he'd be left vulnerable to an attack from the other two.

Rhys panted as he ran, lifted his baseball bat in a double-handed grip, and wound back.

When he got closer, he swung for the nearest of the three diseased. They didn't see him coming. The bat cracked the thing's skull and its legs buckled instantly. The creature hit the tiled floor so hard it shook the ground beneath Rhys' feet. It fell lifeless and blood drooled from its wide mouth.

Rhys fought for breath, turned to the other two, and stopped dead.

The man had jumped to life, kicked one of the diseased to the ground, and introduced the other one to the business end of his axe.

The heavy swing ended in a wet crack, which split the diseased's head in two. It parted it down the middle and sprayed blood up in a jet from its crown. The other one got up and ran at him again. He threw a sideways swing at it and the axe's head dug into the creature's neck.

The second one fell and its head flopped limp. Despite the dark-red axe wound, it kicked and spun on the spot, driven by some semblance of consciousness that spurred it on to reach out at the man.

The man's trainers squeaked as he moved across the

rapidly dampening floor, and he delivered another blow to the diseased's head. A wet crack, similar to moments before, echoed through the small alcove at the front of Building Thirteen.

Then silence.

A second later, the man stood up straight and grinned. "That put the fucker's lights out."

The spilled blood released the rotten smell of the diseased and hot saliva rained down the back of Rhys' throat. He'd never get used to the reek, especially from creatures that shouldn't have started to decompose yet. "If I'd have known you were this competent," he said, "I would have left you to it."

The man stared, his penetrating blue eyes cold and intense.

A chill ran through Rhys as they stood in silence.

A distant sound of people cut through the tension. Rhys turned around but couldn't see them. Banging and shouting, they persisted. When he looked back at the man, the man pointed a thumb at the building they stood in front of.

"It's the people trapped in there," he said, his voice low.

The metal shutters muted their desperation. If Rhys stepped any farther away, he wouldn't have been able to hear them at all. "How many people across the city are crying for help right now do you think?"

The man shrugged. "Probably all of them. I'm sure they don't realise no one can hear them." He shook his head and snorted a humourless laugh. "If only they knew what was out here; they wouldn't be so fucking keen to leave." He thrust a hand at Rhys. "Oscar."

Rhys took the offered hand and winced at the death grip he received. Even the man's hands had thick muscles running through them. "Rhys."

Despite Oscar's heavy scrutiny, Rhys couldn't ignore the people in the building. When he tuned into it, his guts churned and what little strength he had in his body drained from him. People cried and shouted. People banged. It was like listening to people trapped below the deck of a sinking ship. All the commotion in the world couldn't free them, yet they persisted.

A shake of his head and Rhys shut them out. When he looked at Oscar, he said, "We *need* to get out of here. They may be muted in that building, but if the crowd by the bridge hears them, we're fucked."

Oscar didn't reply, but when Rhys ran down the alleyway next to the building, he heard the sound of Oscar's footsteps as he followed behind him.

CHAPTER 4

By the time Rhys reached the end of the alley, a stitch cut into his side and drove a sharp pain up beneath his ribs. He slowed down and gripped his ample love handles. He breathed so heavily he couldn't get his words out.

When he looked up at Oscar, the taller and fitter man regarded him with a sneer as if just being in his company was an affront to him. However, he wore a grimace as if he too were in some kind of pain. Rhys looked him up and down but couldn't place where his discomfort came from.

Rhys dropped his hands to his knees, leaned forward, and spoke at the floor. "All right, I'm not very fit, *okay*?"

When he looked back up again, he saw Oscar roll his eyes and shake his head.

"*You* chose to follow me. I didn't ask you to come."

The same cold penetrative stare from just a few minutes ago regarded Rhys, but Oscar still said nothing.

Sweat stood out on Rhys' brow. After he'd wiped it away with the back of his hand, he stood up straight and poked his head from the alley. A look up and down the street and he saw the poles that had shot up along the middle of each road remained. They ran a militant line that prevented any vehicle wider than about a metre from travelling through the city.

From where he stood, Rhys could see the Draw Bridge underground station. The memory of the rats returned—the writhing black carpet, the smell of the dirty animals, their repeated bashing into his feet... A shiver snapped through him.

The dark road surface and poor light meant Rhys missed it on his first glance, but when he did a second sweep of the road, he saw the huge pool of blood no more than a metre away from him. About three metres in diameter, the dark liquid had a slight reflective quality to it.

When Oscar stepped up next to him and peered out of the alleyway, Rhys nodded at the asphalt. "It looks like they left someone to bleed out."

"If they'd have left them to bleed out, there'd be a body. It looks like they attacked a group of people here." At first, Oscar screwed his face up, and then pushed the back of his hand to his nose. "It fucking *stinks*."

The entire city stank. Rhys must have gotten used to it already, but now that Oscar had mentioned it, the strong acidic tang of rot returned to his consciousness and snaked into his sinuses.

"So are you ready to move on yet?" Oscar said.

A few more deep breaths and Rhys shook his head. "I wish I'd never saved you now."

"You didn't save me, son."

Son? They were about the same age. Rhys didn't respond; instead, he looked at the fitter man. The way he stood grabbed Rhys' attention; something seemed odd about him. He raised one of his legs slightly, but why? Maybe he just stood that way. Rhys then looked at the two bottles that hung from his belt. Both had a rag in the top. "What are you, some kind of corny action hero, or something?"

"They're Molotov cocktails," Oscar said. "Petrol bombs."

"I know what Molotov cocktails are."

"You never know when they might come in handy."

Not only did Oscar have the ability to blow up a small vehicle, but his axe could clearly do some serious damage. By comparison, a baseball bat seemed pretty pathetic. Sure, Rhys had a good swing on him, but the way Oscar had killed those diseased earlier... Blood still dripped from the axe's sharp blade.

"What are you doing here, Oscar? Why are you heading into the city rather than away from it?"

"I could ask you the same, you know?"

"And so what if you did? I don't have anything to hide."

Silence.

"The mother of my child and my best friend are both trapped in those towers. I need to get to The Alpha Tower so I can deactivate the city's defence system and let the people out." He pulled Vicky's security card from his pocket and showed it to Oscar. Rhys noticed the larger man's eyes widen before he added, "This will get me into the tower, but I need to find a card with a higher clearance level to override the defence system once I'm in there. I'm hoping there'll be one inside. When I release the shutters, shit's going to get real."

Rhys cringed at his own words. He never said 'shit's going to get real'. Besides, if shit were to get real, Oscar had less to worry about than he did. Oscar looked like a man who could cope with real shit.

Clearly lost in thought, a deep frown on his face, Oscar said, "The mother of your child? So your wife? Your partner?"

"We're not together anymore."

"*Why* are you saving her then?"

Irritation spiked inside of Rhys; of all the things Oscar could ask... A deep breath, and the rush of rot smothered him again. "I'm doing it for my son." Rhys removed his photo of Flynn from his top pocket and showed it to Oscar.

The smile looked odd on Oscar's otherwise stern face, like he'd done it for effect rather than because he actually gave a shit. The guy obviously didn't have children.

"He lives with his mum most of the time, so he's used to having her around. He's only six and he wants me to make sure she's okay. I need to do everything within my power to make that happen. If nothing else, I want to be able to look him in the eyes and say I tried to save her. I want him to know I did everything I could."

A shrill scream shot through the city. Rhys' breath caught in his throat and he froze as he waited for the next sound.

Another cry, farther away this time.

When Rhys looked at Oscar, the taller man's blue eyes showed no hint of fear. He poked his head out of the alleyway again. When he pulled back in, he said, "I need to save someone too."

The icy coolness of the man made him impossible to read. Just being around him sent a deep unease through Rhys, and he shifted on the spot as if uncomfortable in his own skin.

"It's my younger brother," Oscar said. "He has Down's."

The words were a gut punch and Rhys shook his head. What an arsehole for doubting him. "I'm sorry to hear that, man."

"You're sorry that he has Down's syndrome?"

"No, well yes, but I'm sorry that he's trapped. You must be really worried."

Oscar shrugged. "I trained a lot with him. He's probably better equipped to deal with this than most of the other people on this godforsaken island." Oscar looked at Rhys' portly stomach before he made eye contact with him again. "He works in Tower Eighteen. He organises the internal mail. It's a bit of an outdated job, and they probably don't need him there at all. He spends most of his days emptying the bins. It really fucks me off because he may have Down's, but he's not fucking useless. He's probably more capable than half of the people he works with. I wish they'd give him a try at doing a better job. They don't need to create a position for him. He doesn't *need* their charity."

The glaze of tears reflected off Oscar's eyes and he cleared his throat. "He's the most wonderful and kindest person I know. I'd die for him."

"You may have to." The words left Rhys' mouth before he'd thought about them. When Oscar looked at him with a hard frown, Rhys' face burned and he dropped his eyes to the Superman Lego watch on his wrist. "Whatever happens, we need to be off this island in less than five hours."

A tilt of his head to one side and Oscar said, "Why's that?"

Rhys' breath had levelled out so he stood up straighter and filled his lungs with the stench around him. He coughed several times and came close to heaving before he said, "This place is set to blow. There's a countdown before the entire city incinerates. There's less than five hours left."

A deeper frown crushed Oscar's face and he ran a hand through his short black hair. "Fuck! We don't have much time. I'm coming with you to The Alpha Tower. If you have a way to get inside, then you'll need me. Without me, you won't last more than five minutes."

The pros far outweighed the cons. The man could fight. In fact, the man was a machine. "I don't want you getting shitty about my fitness though. I *wish* I was fitter, but there's nothing I can do about it now, so the last thing I need is you bitching about it, okay? I'd rather go on my own, if that's the case."

Oscar's jaw tightened and his eyes pinched at the sides. Crow's feet spread round to his temples. "So if you're doing this for your boy, where is he now?"

"Did you hear the car horn when you were fighting the diseased off?"

"Yeah."

"That was my friend. I asked her to make some noise so the diseased by the drawbridge would remain there. The last thing we needed was that mob seeing you. If they'd have run over, there's no way I would have been able to get into the city."

"Are you trying to give me a bollocking or is there more to this story?"

"No… sorry, yes there's more—the person in the car has him with her right now. She agreed to stay outside the city while I came in."

"She sounds like the sensible one." Before Rhys could respond, Oscar added, "She must be a good friend to trust her with the life of your child."

Anxiety gnawed at Rhys' gut, but he nodded through it. The sound of his own uncertainty shook his words. "Yeah, she is."

"You've known her long?"

A slight pause and Rhys looked up at Oscar. His voice cracked when he said, "A day. I'd never met her before all of this shit happened, but she saved me. She kept me alive when everyone else was panicking and she's the reason I managed to rescue my son in the first place."

Silence.

"Just say it," Rhys said.

"It's awfully trusting of you."

"Look, in the past twelve or so hours, she's done more for me than any other person in my entire life. I trust her one hundred percent."

Again, Oscar remained silent.

Rhys ground his jaw and looked the man up and down. He trusted Vicky a damn sight more than he trusted Oscar.

CHAPTER 5

R hys walked up the middle of the road and hung his right hand down so he could hit each pole as he passed them. The contact made a quiet *ting* that no one any farther away than Oscar could hear. A gentle tingle remained on his fingertips after each tap.

The sound also broke through the background hum of the infected. Surrounded on all sides by the distant groans and moans of the diseased, Rhys needed to distract himself in some way. With panic balled in his chest, the slight sound and sensation kept it at bay.

When a scream, louder than the others, shot out of an alleyway to their right, Rhys dropped into a defensive crouch and raised his bat. Oscar did the same but the quick movement made him stumble. He remained on his feet but held his right leg like it hurt. With his axe raised, he stared in the direction of the sound.

As Rhys watched the alleyway, he gulped. It did nothing to rehydrate his throat or clear the stale taste in his mouth. Very little drink and a diet of sugary snacks had left a funky layer of fur on his tongue.

After a minute or so, Oscar, who had relaxed his right leg again, spoke in a whisper. "They're not coming. Let's go."

The line of densely packed buildings along either side of the street created an alleyway about every twenty metres. Dark and mysterious, each one had the potential to send a stream of infected toward them.

Rhys' eyeballs stung as he continued to look around. A quick glance and he saw that Oscar watched their environment with the same intense focus.

"She's a good person, you know," Rhys said.

Oscar continued to scan his surroundings. "Huh?"

"The woman who's looking after Flynn; she's a good person. She went out of her way to help me find him. She could have saved her skin and left me to die, but she didn't."

"I'm not saying she's a bad person. I was merely observing your trusting nature. It's a quality."

What a condescending arsehole! Rhys didn't reply.

A sharp crack came from an alleyway on their left. Both men turned in its direction. The fear inside of Rhys grew wings and beat in his chest like it wanted out.

After a few seconds, nothing had happened so the men looked at one another and moved on again.

Oscar rolled his neck from side to side and turned circles with his shoulders. "I'm not good at trusting people. The only person I trust is my brother. He's got my back and I have his."

"You've not told me his name yet."

"What does it matter?"

Rhys raised his hands in defence. "Sorry, mate; I'm just making conversation."

Oscar watched Rhys for a few seconds before he returned his focus to their environment. "Alan. His name's Alan."

Rhys nodded and looked up the street. Smoke rose from a tower at the far end. "What the fuck's happening there?"

A squint against the sun and Oscar looked to where Rhys pointed. "Dunno, but that's the third tower I've seen on fire. Poor fuckers. How are they supposed to get out of a burning building with those *stupid* fucking shutters penning them in?" His eyes lost focus. "I heard people screaming from the last one I saw like that. I could hear the popping of windows and crackling of a bonfire inside. That one looks like it's well and truly gone though. Burned out already. I doubt *anyone's* left alive in there."

The damp weight of grief swelled inside Rhys as he watched it for a few more seconds. When he looked up, he saw The Alpha Tower through a gap between two buildings. A tug on Oscar's sleeve and he pointed at an alleyway that led toward it. "Let's go down there. It looks clear, and if there are people still burning alive in that tower, I'd rather not experience their suffering."

Oscar's chest rose with a deep inhalation and he dipped a stoic nod. "Good idea."

RHYS RAN HIS FINGERS ALONG THE ROUGH BRICK WALL TO HIS left. Had he not had his bat, he would have been able to touch the wall on the right at the same time. Most of the alleyways were the same in Summit City; the buildings had been built as closely together as they could have been. Efficiency must have been the number-one priority when building the place—aesthetics clearly didn't come very high on the list.

Rhys should have watched the exit up ahead, but he turned around to look at Oscar and his slight limp. When he made eye contact with the man, Oscar snapped his shoulders up in a sharp shrug. "What are you looking at?"

"You look like you've hurt yourself," Rhys said.

Oscar replied with the same aggression. "What are you talking about?"

Before Rhys could elaborate and maybe ask Oscar to lift his trouser leg, the big man pointed in front of them. "Watch up ahead, yeah? *Anything* could come down this alley at any second."

The guy obviously had something to hide. Was he bit? Surely he would have changed by now if he'd been bitten. Rhys turned and focused on the end of the alley. They'd discuss his injury again at some point. Until then, he'd have to keep one eye on the lunatic with the axe.

Other than the sound of their footsteps, they kept it quiet in the alley so they'd get a heads up on the diseased. The sooner they heard the clumsy beat of a stampede, the more time they'd have to react. Rhys even held his breath for as long as he could to make it quieter.

With The Alpha Tower in sight, and no sign of the diseased, Rhys tensed up more than ever before. As the distant cries of fury screamed through the city, Rhys swallowed another dry gulp. Something would change. No way could they be so lucky as to walk straight through the city without incident.

"I need to get to tower Seventy-two and tower Twenty-one," Rhys said. His voice echoed off the close walls. "I need to let Larissa and Dave know what's going to happen so they can be ready when the shutters come up. It's going to be insane. They need to be prepared."

Oscar didn't reply.

"Which tower did you say your brother was in?"

The enclosed space added a resonance to Oscar's deep voice. "Twenty-four. Although I'm not going to go to him. They treat him like an idiot at work. Like he's dumb. I think if I go there, I'll spend all of my time trying to persuade them to let me talk to him. It'll be easier for us to open the shutters first. I'll go and get him afterwards."

As he neared the end of the alleyway, Rhys slowed down. The hot sun warmed his face when he peered out. The alley opened into a mini square. Shops ran down two sides and a road bordered it.

When Oscar stepped out behind him, Rhys moved a step away. If the virus ran through his veins, Rhys had to have a head start on him at least.

Oscar squinted as he looked around. "It's a shame we can't drive. We'd be in and out of this city in no time if it weren't for those stupid fucking poles."

A huge open space without a single diseased in sight, although their sound still rode the light breeze; Rhys shook his head. "Where the fuck are they?"

"That's not a question I'd be asking. The last thing we need is for those infected freaks to turn up."

"But what if they're all in one massive herd and we run into that?"

"Herd? What are they, cows?"

Rhys rolled his eyes. The quickest way to The Alpha Tower involved going straight across the square.

As if he'd read his mind, Oscar pointed in the direction they needed to travel. "I don't know about you, but I think we should take route one. How much time do we have left?"

Rhys looked at Flynn's watch. "Just over four and a half hours."

"I say we go straight for it." Oscar looked Rhys up and down and raised his eyebrows. "You got any more running in you, princess?"

What a dick! Aches sat deep in nearly every muscle, but Rhys nodded anyway; hopefully he did. Besides, it seemed that Oscar should be the one worried about the run; Rhys didn't have a bad leg.

"Okay, well, follow me."

The big man darted out into the square and Rhys followed as fast as he could. Although Oscar moved with a strange gait, like he still had a problem with his leg, Rhys lost ground to him instantly.

Both of them searched their environment as they ran. They could get surrounded on all sides. Rhys shook the thought from his head. It didn't bear thinking about.

Once in the middle of the square, Oscar ran backwards so he could face Rhys. He looked to be in pain, but he tried to smile through it. "You okay?"

Rhys chased his breath. It felt like his lungs had shrunk, but he nodded.

~

AT THE OTHER SIDE OF THE SQUARE, RHYS RUBBED HIS EYES. It did little to relieve the sting from tiredness and the sweat that had run into them. He blinked repeatedly as he followed Oscar down the alleyway that led in the direction of The Alpha Tower.

The sounds of the diseased—even the faraway sounds— had died down. Oscar slowed in front of Rhys, and Rhys seized the opportunity to walk. He took greedy gulps of air as he did so.

Neither man spoke as they moved along and the sound of Rhys' breathing drowned out their footsteps.

When they neared the end, Oscar turned to Rhys. "How are we doing for time?"

A check of his watch and Rhys gave Oscar the thumbs up.

A quick smile and Oscar stepped out into the next street.

Rhys followed.

Both men froze.

In front of them, packing the road from wall to wall, were what looked to be hundreds—if not a thousand—of the diseased milling about. It seemed that with nothing to chase, they'd fallen into a docile state.

The acrid smell of them hung so thick Rhys could taste it. Before he had time to dive back into the alleyway, a heave rose up from his guts and came out as a deep retch.

As one, the mob snapped their heads in Rhys and Oscar's direction.

CHAPTER 6

R hys focused on Oscar's broad back as he ran up the alley, away from the mob. The clumsy stampede thundered behind them. Growls, yowls, and cries all headed for the enclosed space. Their phlegmy rattle ran an undertone through the cacophony of fury.

When he glanced behind, Rhys saw the start of the pack. So driven to get at the pair, they fought one another to be at the front. The pandemonium created a bottleneck that jammed them tight. It gave Rhys and Oscar the slightest advantage as the diseased shoved and pushed one another to get free of the congestion.

Oscar pulled farther away. In his haste, he made no effort to disguise his obvious limp. No matter how deep Rhys dug though, his legs wouldn't move any faster. He didn't even have the breath to call after him.

When Rhys turned around again, the diseased at the front had made it clear of the bottleneck and ran down the alleyway. They crashed into the walls on either side. Many of them fell to the floor and were trampled by the ones behind them. Rhys faced the front again, dropped his head, and gave everything he had to his escape.

Seconds later, as the diseased gained on them, their smell hit Rhys. It turned the air sour and stars swam in his vision. He had no choice but to take deep breaths of the rotten air to fill his tight lungs.

When Oscar exited the alley and disappeared from sight, Rhys' legs buckled and he stumbled. It didn't matter that he'd see him again in a few seconds, he couldn't see him now.

Rhys pushed on and shot out of the alleyway. Oscar ran down the road and Rhys followed him. Hopefully he had a plan.

When he got closer to a car park, Rhys saw the big man's intention. He wanted to scream but he had no breath left.

Unlike the other multi-storey Rhys had entered with Vicky, this one stood on its own.

Oscar ran into it and Rhys shook his head. *Fuck!* He gritted his teeth, pushed harder, and followed him in. It had to be better than going his own way.

Rhys lost sight of Oscar again, but he heard the stairwell's door slam shut and headed for it.

The low-ceilinged car park amplified Rhys' heavy foot-steps as he followed. By the time he'd reached the stairwell door, it had increased the volume of the slathering, moaning mob behind.

Rhys turned around and momentarily froze. Without the tight alleyway to hold them back, the numbers seemed to have trebled. A mass of bleeding eyes, snapping jaws, and flailing limbs rushed at him. Packed tightly together, they looked like one enraged entity.

Rhys ripped the door open and ran into the cool stairwell. His lungs burned and his head spun as he chased Oscar's footsteps up the stairs. The place reeked of damp concrete. It made the air heavier and harder to breathe.

The pain in his tired legs had gotten worse the farther he ran. The concrete staircase set his weak muscles on fire as he pushed on.

"Come on, Rhys. Hurry up, man."

The sound of Oscar's voice spurred Rhys on. A surge of strength rushed through him.

"You can do it."

"I *can't*," Rhys cried.

The door smashed open behind him and the sound of splintering wood ripped up the staircase. It sounded like they'd knocked the thing clean off its hinges.

"You'd *better*; otherwise, you're fucked."

The patter of footsteps that chased him up the stairs turned into a continuous hum. The concrete stairs shook as if they'd collapse at any minute.

"When you get up here," Oscar called out over the reverberating thunder of hundreds of diseased, "I'm sending a Molotov down behind you. Be ready for it, and hurry the fuck up."

The same stitch Rhys felt earlier returned with a vengeance and tore at his ribs like it could crack them open. Rhys saved his breath and hoped Oscar would hold off on the Molotov until he'd reached the top.

When Rhys made it up the next flight of stairs, he saw Oscar. He had the door open for him to run straight out. The monsters sounded close, but Rhys didn't look.

He passed Oscar, who had the Molotov in his hand. A hungry flame chewed up the rag and gave off black smoke. As Rhys sprinted through the open doorway into the bright sun, he heard a smash followed by a loud *whoosh*!

Oscar sent the second Molotov after the first. It set the air alive with shrill cries of agony as the creatures burned.

The beat of their footsteps stopped.

Before Rhys could even begin to catch his breath, Oscar sprinted past him and headed for the down ramp normally used by cars. He called over his shoulder, "The fire's slowed them down, but we have to go *now* if we're to get away."

A deep heave and Rhys vomited what little he had in his stomach. The chocolate from earlier burned on its way out and left an acidic imprint on the back of his throat. Rhys spat several times and followed Oscar. The big man's limp looked worse than ever, but Rhys decided that if he'd been bitten, he would have most assuredly turned by now.

WHEN THEY GOT TO THE FIRST FLOOR, OSCAR SHOWED RHYS to stop with a raised palm.

Rhys stopped dead and panted as he stared at the big man.

With a finger pressed to his lips, Oscar pointed at the ground.

Although he couldn't see them, Rhys heard the clumsy rush of the diseased as they continued to enter the car park on the floor below them.

Oscar brushed his hair back from his forehead and his cheeks puffed out when he exhaled. "Fuck it! How the fuck are we going to get out?"

While the larger man paced, Rhys linked his hands behind his head and gasped for breath. Sweat stuck his clothes to his skin as he walked over to the edge of the car park and peered out. They were at least seven metres from the ground; about four metres too high to jump. However, with the diseased both above and below them, did they have any other choice? Then he saw it.

It took a second to get Oscar's attention as he paced up and down. When the big man saw him, Rhys waved him over and pointed at the green street lamp by the corner of the car park. After another couple of deep breaths, he said, "We could shimmy down that."

The only response Oscar offered was to scowl at the street lamp and then look behind them.

"Do you have any better ideas?" Rhys said.

Another look behind and Oscar's face relaxed. He shook his head.

WHEN OSCAR JOINED RHYS NEAR THE STREET LAMP, RHYS took several calming breaths and wiped his hands on his trousers. They remained clammy.

"Go on then," Oscar said, "hurry up."

As if to highlight his point, the sound of the door at the top of the stairwell cracked open and the screams from the diseased emerged with the heavy tattoo of their feet.

Rhys swallowed, his throat so dry it pinched, and he nearly vomited again. The wall around the car park stood about a metre tall. Rhys hopped up on it and dropped into a squat. His legs shook and his world spun when he looked down. A metre of fresh air separated him and the street lamp. He only had one chance to make it. One final deep breath and he leaned forward. His stomach lurched as he fell toward it.

The paint on the thick pole coated it like a rubber film. When Rhys caught it, he stopped instantly. He couldn't help but smile when he looked up at Oscar. "I made it."

"I can see." Oscar glanced over his shoulder. "Now *move* so I can follow."

Rhys wrapped his legs around the pole and started his controlled slide to the bottom. Centimetres at a time, he eased himself closer to the ground.

Once he'd gone past the first floor, Rhys looked into the lower level. The diseased continued to rush into the car park, the line of them as dense as ever. In their single-minded pursuit of their prey, all of them concentrated on the stairwell. Even when some of them fell to the floor, they got back up and didn't lose focus. They were oblivious to their meal ticket escaping right next to them.

Seconds after Rhys jumped off the pole, Oscar leaped onto it. The tall lamp swayed as if it would snap under the man's considerable weight. When it held, Oscar shimmied down it.

At the bottom, Oscar jumped to the ground and failed to hide his awkward landing on his bad leg. He then glared at Rhys before he sprinted away from the car park.

A deep inhale and Rhys' lungs felt like they could pop at any moment. One more breath and he followed after Oscar.

AFTER THEY'D DUCKED INTO AN ALLEYWAY A FEW HUNDRED metres from the car park, Oscar and Rhys stopped.

Rhys dropped his hands to his knees and hunched over. His navel pulled up into his ribcage as he chugged on the air around him. Fire burned in his guts, and seconds later, he vomited acidic bile as thick as glue.

He looked up to see disdain spread across Oscar's face. A wipe of his mouth with the back of his sleeve, and Rhys said, "I've never pretended to be fit." He heaved again but didn't vomit this time. "We got away; that's the best I can do at the moment."

"We need to find a better way to travel around this city," Oscar said. "We can't carry on like this. We're lucky they haven't caught us yet. I need to stay alive so I can rescue Adam."

Rhys looked up at his new friend. "*Adam*?"

A slight flush ran across Oscar's cheeks before his usual stoic expression replaced it. "Alan."

"You said Adam."

Oscar stepped forward and loomed over Rhys. He shook when he said, "Why the *fuck* would I say Adam?"

"I don't know, but you did."

A shake of his head and Oscar shot a blast of air from his mouth as if to dismiss Rhys' comment. "I think all that running has gone to your head, princess. Why don't you focus on getting your breath back so we can get the fuck out of here? Waiting for you is going to get me killed."

He'd definitely said Adam. He'd definitely gotten his own brother's name wrong.

CHAPTER 7

Oscar had definitely said Adam, not Alan. If he'd have gotten someone—anyone else's name wrong, Rhys could let it slide, but his *brother*…? And not only his brother, but—according to him—the most important person in his world.

A trickle of sweat ran from Rhys' armpit down his side. Dryness spread to every part of his mouth and into his throat. The nausea that only heat and thirst could bring tightened its dizzying grip on him.

With each alleyway came the potential for yet another ambush, so Rhys wiped his brow and watched every one they passed. The occasional look behind showed him that the diseased from the multi-storey car park had yet to pick up their trail. *Thank god.*

A glance at Oscar, and Rhys saw he walked with what seemed to be a more pronounced limp than before. The run must have taken its toll on him. Rhys checked his brow—no sweat. His eyes—they seemed clear. The slight pull back of his lips—he couldn't see that either. If he had been bitten and would turn into one of the diseased, he hid it well. But if he hadn't been bitten, why did he go to so much effort to hide it?

Although Oscar didn't look back at Rhys, he wore his usual scowl. It said 'fuck off' and 'don't fucking talk to me'. Not that Rhys cared about that. "So how old is your brother?"

"What?" The one syllable boomed from Oscar's mouth like a cannonball.

"Your brother, how old is he?"

Oscar drew a deep breath that lifted his large chest. "I don't want to talk about him anymore."

Convenient! Is that because you're worried you might forget his name again? Rhys kept the thought to himself.

"I've already let you too far into my world. Why don't you just stay focused on what's going on around us before we get jumped again, yeah?"

The man may have been much larger than him, but he couldn't silence Rhys with aggression. As they walked, Rhys held eye contact with him and let his hand hit the pillars. Each gentle *ting* lifted Oscar's shoulders closer to his ears. Rhys hit each one harder than the last.

A tut, and Oscar spun away to look in the other direction.

Rhys looked around too. Tower Seventy-two, the tower that he used to work in and currently contained Larissa and most of his colleagues, stood on the horizon. The large phallus, an industrial-looking stalagmite with its armoured shell, looked exactly the same as the buildings that surrounded it. The large pods that used to be towers littered the entire city as if dropped by an invading alien army. They could almost be huge hives set to open up at any point and release a violent and bloodthirsty race of beings.

A distant scream ran ice down Rhys' spine. *Maybe aliens would be easier to deal with than those fuckers.*

Not only did the shutters cast an otherworldly look over the city, but they also muted the sounds of the people contained within the buildings. An eerie stillness hung in the air like low-lying fog; it felt like walking through a graveyard.

Rhys hit the next pole a little too hard. The *ting* rang out and the tips of his fingers throbbed from the contact.

Oscar looked at him and Rhys dropped his attention to the ground. Dark bloodstains had sunk into the asphalt. Then Rhys saw something pink and his stomach twinged. He pointed down. "A severed ear, look. A small, severed ear. It must have belonged to either a tiny adult or, more likely…" he paused as the memory of the school bus massacre choked him. He cleared his throat and finally said, "A child."

Oscar glanced at the ear; his face twisted with his own displeasure rather than any kind of concern for the victim. When he looked up again, he pointed at a building and said, "Fuck, another one."

The lump of grief remained wedged in Rhys' throat when he looked to where Oscar had pointed—another tower burned. Dark smoke like the kind released from burning plastic seeped through the gaps in the armoured plates. "If the smoke's that thick," Rhys said, "fuck knows what it's like *inside* the tower."

A shake of his head and Oscar's shoulders slumped. "It's a damn waste of people. Why are there so many fires?"

Rhys remained quiet as he watched the tall man. Something in the way he reacted rang false; almost as if it were an act, like he couldn't really give a fuck if they burned or not. He had the external sheen of a psychopath well practiced in pleasantries.

When they got closer to the building, Rhys heard a raspy voice call out into the street. "I can't breathe."

A series of coughs came from the man, then he said again, "I can't fucking breathe."

Heavy gasps and the voice came again. Each word slightly quieter than the last. "I can't breathe. I can't breathe. I can't…"

Rhys and Oscar glanced at one another, but neither spoke as the man's voice faded away.

The thuds of tired fists beat against the other side of the shutters.

Then another voice, this time that of a woman. "I'm too young to die. What about my children?"

Rhys' chest tightened and his eyes stung with tears. If Oscar asked, it was because of the thick smoke. A deep frown darkened Rhys' view of the building as he listened to the weakened female voice mewl, "I can't breathe."

Neither of them had called for help. They'd clearly given up on that pipe dream.

"I hope Larissa and Dave are okay," Rhys said as he fought to get his words out past his grief.

When he glanced at Oscar, he saw the large man stare at the burning building. Crow's feet spread away from the edges of his narrowed eyes. A watery glaze covered his eyeballs. The rare glimpse of emotion ran another wave of sadness through Rhys. A deep exhale did little to banish it, so Rhys looked at his Superman watch and said, "We have just over four hours left."

Oscar didn't reply.

The look at the watch ran anxiety through Rhys. He removed the walkie-talkie from his pocket and flicked it on.

Oscar stared at it. "What the fuck are you *doing*?"

Rhys depressed the talk button on the side. It banished the quiet hiss that came from the speaker. "Hi, it's me. Can you hear me?"

After another glance around, Oscar turned back to Rhys. "Turn it off. You'll make too much noise."

"I'll whisper."

"You'll still make too much noise."

Before Rhys could press the button and try again, he heard Vicky's voice. "Hi."

Rhys' arm shook and his voice wavered. "How's my boy doing?"

He felt Oscar's intense scrutiny burn into the side of his face.

Vicky spoke in a soft tone. "He's good. We're both good. It's all quiet here. Well, I say quiet; the diseased are still waiting on the other side of the bridge, thinking they can get across. Stupid fuckers. Hopefully they'll be gone when you come back. How are things with you?"

After a pause to look at Oscar, the man's icy glare coming back at him with interest, Rhys shrugged. "I'm doing fine. I'm making good progress."

Oscar tutted, shook his head, and looked away.

"Anyway, I don't want to run the battery down. I just needed to check that everything's all right. I'll contact you again soon, okay?"

"Okay," Vicky said.

"I love you, Flynn."

"Love you too, Daddy."

Grief weakened Rhys as he switched the walkie-talkie off. They both sounded calm and some of the tension left his body. Oscar may doubt her, but she can be trusted. *Fuck what Oscar thought.*

As the pair moved off, Rhys wedged the large walkie-talkie back in his pocket. Once he'd finished, he lifted his head. Oscar still stared at him.

"I dunno why the fuck I'm doing this," Rhys said. "The

boy's mum has been a bitch to me for ages now. I should have just left her in the city and got as far away from here as possible."

Oscar's words lost their sharpness. "Yeah, but every little boy needs his mummy, eh?"

The moment of sensitivity caught Rhys off guard and it took a second for him to ask, "Do you have kids?"

Oscar shook his head and looked back at the tower in front of them. "No."

Rhys looked the tall man up and down and a deep unease sat in his gut. Everything about him seemed to be covering up a lie.

When Rhys saw it, he stopped dead.

Oscar stopped too. "What? What is it?"

Rhys pointed to a shop on the other side of the road.

For a few seconds, Oscar looked from Rhys to the shop and back to Rhys again. "A bike shop, so what? We can't get inside."

Rhys removed the card Vicky had given him from his top pocket and waved it in the air. "We can with this."

A crocodilian smile spread across Oscar's wide face. "You fucking beauty," the big man said. He gave Rhys a playful punch on the top of his shoulder. It knocked Rhys back a couple of steps. "Kept that one quiet, didn't ya? With bikes, we can get to The Alpha Tower and back with no problem. That babysitter of yours has proven to be pretty darn handy."

Despite the urge to rub his now sore shoulder, Rhys resisted. "She's a good woman!"

The smile remained on Oscar's wide face. "I can't speak to that, but she's certainly helped by giving you access to most of Summit City."

What did it matter if Oscar could speak to it or not? He

didn't need Oscar's approval. Rhys nodded in the direction of the cycle shop. "Come on, let's go."

CHAPTER 8

Rhys's hand shook when he held it near the card reader. Reluctance tugged on his muscles as if his body knew something he didn't. He looked over his shoulder at the quiet city behind him. The diseased from the car park would be with them at some point. The longer they waited around, the more chance they'd have of bumping into them. He swiped the card and watched the red light on the reader turn green.

Several clicks as the shutter mechanism came to life and the steel barrier rolled up from the top. Made from horizontal strips of brushed steel much like the metal used to protect the towers, the bottom of the shutter lifted from the ground.

Although the process wasn't slow, impatience ran through Rhys and he tapped his foot as he waited. He chewed on his lip and scanned the city behind him again. "Come on, this is taking *too* fucking long."

Oscar ran a more languid surveillance of their surroundings and said nothing.

The sun set on the horizon and Rhys glanced at his watch. Just over an hour had passed since he'd left his boy. He drew a deep breath and exhaled hard.

The motors whirred and Rhys cleared his throat as he continued to watch the abandoned city. "Maybe we led every diseased in the city to the car park and they're still there."

Oscar looked back in the direction of the multi-storey and lifted his wide shoulders in a shrug. "As long as they stay there."

When Oscar spoke, Rhys watched him to look for any chink in his façade. The response seemed natural but Oscar also seemed well practiced in the art of deceit. When he'd finally worked out Oscar's angle, he'd be much easier to read. Until then, he'd just have to guess. He didn't have a brother with Down's, that much seemed clear. Or if he did, he wasn't trapped in Summit City, and he wasn't called Alan. As for Oscar's injury…

When Oscar turned back around, Rhys looked away.

After a moment of silence, Rhys looked back at him.

The big man's blue eyes narrowed. "I've been meaning to ask you," he said and looked down, "why the fuck do you have odd trainers on?"

Rhys focused on his feet and wiggled his toes. The sweat between them turned the movement slick. The previously new trainer looked far from that now. Both of them had brown stains from old blood and were scuffed from heavy use. A shrug of his shoulders, and Rhys pointed at the new one. "I found this one in a sports shop when I was leaving the city a few hours ago. After putting it on, I realised the other one would be somewhere in the store cupboard, and we didn't want to hang around to look for it."

The look on Oscar's face said 'you idiot', but he kept his response to himself and turned to look at the shutter. It had lifted high enough for them to enter the shop.

A deep breath did little to settle the butterflies in Rhys' stomach, so he pushed through it and ducked under the barrier as it continued to rise. Oscar let him lead the way and followed him in.

All of the shop's displays and decor had bike themes. A huge wheel dominated the centre of the space. About two metres wide, it held at least thirty bikes and spun to allow customers to view the stock.

Although they led to a private area, the stairs in the corner of the shop had been made to look like cogs. The counter rested on top of a large set of replica handlebars. Made from glass, it had been filled with fireworks. Even the cycle clothing hung from hangers hooked over wheels suspended from the ceiling like model aeroplanes. The entire place smelled of oil and rubber.

Rhys walked to the back of the shop with Oscar at his side. From the corner of his eye, he caught movement beneath a pile of clothes and raised his baseball bat. Oscar did the same with his axe.

A girl emerged. Scruffy and no more than about five feet tall, she held a firework in one hand and a lighter in the other. The firework shook at the end of her outstretched arm.

Rhys stepped forward and then froze when she sparked the lighter at him.

"I'll send this firework into your fucking *face* if you take another step closer." Spittle shot from her mouth as she spoke.

Rhys raised his hands. "Calm down, love, we don't mean you any harm."

"Like fuck. If you didn't mean me any harm, why the fuck have I been locked in this shitty shop for so long? I don't know what's going on, but you're *not* keeping me in here any longer."

With the firework still pointed at the pair, she made her way over to the large cycle display in the centre of the shop.

All the while, she kept her eyes on Rhys and Oscar. "I expect you to stay there while I get the fuck out of here."

When Oscar stepped forward, she thrust the firework in his direction. Her skin flushed red and her eyes widened. "I *mean* it."

"Easy, princess," said Oscar, his voice much kinder with her than it had ever been with Rhys. "All I wanted to say is it's rough out there."

She glanced down to where she'd been hiding. "Anything's got to be better than sweating it out in here."

Oscar winced. "I'm not sure that's true."

"He's right," Rhys said.

Another lunge with the firework, and the girl shouted through gritted teeth. "Stay the fuck back or I'll light this thing."

Rhys and Oscar looked at one another before Rhys said, "But you need to listen to us. It's dangerous out there."

She jabbed the firework at him again. "Back!"

After he'd stepped back, Rhys continued, "There are zombies out there."

The girl stopped and tilted her head to one side. "Do I look like I was born yesterday?"

Rhys wanted to argue, but she had the lighter dangerously close to the firework's fuse. With one hand, she tugged on a bike. All of the other bikes rattled as she fought to liberate the one she'd chosen. Instead of watching the girl, Rhys looked out into the street. She'd made enough noise to bring hell down on top of them.

When she'd pulled the bike free, she jumped onto the saddle. "Don't you *dare* try to follow me."

"Just listen to us," Rhys said.

A spark of the lighter, and the girl lit the fuse. The touch paper hissed and she threw the firework down. Rhys ducked behind the counter and Oscar crouched behind the stairs.

A loud shriek and the firework shot across the floor before it exploded close to Oscar. Rhys' ears rang from the sound.

When he stood back up again, he watched the girl as she raced from the shop. With the bike flick-flacking between her legs, she called over her shoulder, "You fucking arseholes. Fuck you and whatever it is you're doing to this fucking city."

Rhys looked at Oscar and held the security card up.

Oscar nodded.

In three quick steps, Rhys arrived at the control panel and swiped his card through it. As the metal shutter whirred, he watched the girl ride down the street, his heart heavy for her fate.

Before the shutter had closed completely, Rhys ducked down and looked through the gap at the bottom. Six diseased shot from an alleyway at a full sprint. They must have heard the bang. They crashed hard into the girl, which knocked both her and her bike to the ground.

Her scream rang through the quiet city. It was then replaced with a gargled sound as she choked on her own blood.

Just as the shutter closed fully, she fell silent and Rhys sighed. "Poor girl."

"*Stupid* fucking girl more like," Oscar said. "She's better off dead than dragging us down."

As much as Rhys wanted to berate the man, he had to agree with him. The girl would have hindered any chance they had of survival. Shame she had to go out like that though.

CHAPTER 9

The pair spent about the next fifteen minutes in the shop. The first thing they did was pick bikes. Before they'd entered, anything with two wheels would have done. Once faced with a large choice, they became a lot pickier.

Oscar had found a small amount of petrol and turned a water bottle into another Molotov cocktail. He tore a rag off one of the shop's own branded t-shirts that had 'COGS' written across it in capital letters. He stuffed it into the bottle.

Rhys had gone on a search for bags to fill with fireworks and found a stash of energy drinks. The disgusting things stank, tasted like bleach, and dehydrated him; on the plus side, he vibrated with so much nervous energy he felt like he could outrun a racehorse. The jagged anxiety seemed like a small price to pay for the renewed vigour.

After he'd taken a lighter from the box on the side, Rhys threw one at Oscar. He then slipped his new rucksack—heavy with fireworks—onto his back and wheeled the mountain bike he'd chosen to the card reader that would let them out. "You ready?"

Before Oscar said anything, Rhys sniffed the air. The

familiar tang of rot hung heavy. He screwed his nose up and pressed a finger to his lips.

The cold shutter stung the side of his face when he leaned into it and listened. The rank smell increased tenfold with the slight move forward and sent hot saliva down the back of his throat. His pulse galloped when he heard it. Breathing; nothing more, just the collective rattle of wet lungs.

Oscar stared at Rhys with wide eyes and Rhys shook his head.

While he held his breath, Rhys gently leaned his bike against a stand loaded with water bottles. Caffeine and sugar rushed through his system and ran a violent shake through his entire body. His anxiety ratcheted up several notches. Once he'd made sure his bike wouldn't fall, Rhys walked over to the cog-shaped stairs.

At the top, he found a thick steel door. A swipe of his security card popped it from its frame. When he pushed it wide, the hinges creaked.

The low sun dazzled him when he stepped out onto the roof and the heat of the day smothered him like a tight blanket.

A dusting of light stones lay over the three-metre square flat roof. Several large plant pots with a couple of dry and ratty stalks poking up from the soil inside sat at the edge as if ready to be toppled onto the diseased below. The stones crunched beneath Rhys' feet when he walked across it with Oscar by his side.

When they got to the edge and looked down, Rhys' heart jolted and the rock of anxiety in his stomach pinched tighter.

The sea of diseased stretched so far back that Rhys would have struggled to drive a golf ball over the top of them. As he watched them, he shuddered; something about the way they stood around slid an itchy discomfort beneath his skin. Many of them shuffled as if in a perpetual battle to keep their balance, yet most of them seemed relatively calm.

The bloody eyes looked everywhere but up. It would have been easy to assume the monsters were blinded by the thick secretion, but Rhys had been on the receiving end of their attention. Whatever they could see when they faced him was enough to hunt him down with hawk-like focus. Rhys spoke in a whisper, "They're waiting for us to come out."

When Oscar didn't reply, Rhys looked to see him staring out over the crowd. His strong jaw hung loose, and his wide eyes searched the mob.

A shake of his head, and Rhys pulled his hair away from his sticky forehead. "We're fucked, Oscar. We're fucked."

CHAPTER 10

Oscar ground his jaw as he looked out over the diseased mob. "I knew I should have broken that fucking girl's neck."

A chill ran through Rhys as he stared at the big man, who had malice in his cold stare. Sometimes people said things like that and didn't mean it; Oscar's icy tone suggested he not only meant, but he embodied every syllable of it.

Rhys stepped back from the edge of the roof. "It looks like every one of the fuckers from the car park found their way here."

If he'd have stepped back any farther he would have been completely hidden from view, but none of the mob had seen him or Oscar yet, and he couldn't resist the opportunity to watch them. They stood patiently as if waiting in line. It was easy to write these things off as mindless monsters, but they knew what they were doing. They knew Rhys and Oscar were inside the bike shop—or had a sense of it. Maybe they didn't understand why they congregated there, but they had a compulsion to remain there at the very least.

A particularly strong gust of wind cooled the sweat on

Rhys' brow and drove the strong reek of rot into his face. Rhys screwed his nose up against the tang and continued to watch the crowd of diseased.

Some of them caught his eye more than others. A big, fat woman stood near the front. The hole in the side of her neck looked like someone had removed a ten-ounce steak from it. It glistened with a yellowish tinge as if it had started to ooze pus already. Her loose-fitting shirt had been torn open and one of her massive saggy breasts hung from it like an old, half-filled sack.

Behind and to the left of the woman, a small boy bit at the air. No older than Flynn, he looked scared and confused, like he needed direction on who to bite. Half of his hair had been ripped off and revealed a dark-red, tacky scalp. Blood ran down his arm from a deep bite mark in his bicep.

Most of the infected wore suits, but some wore the official uniform of the Summit City police or fire brigade.

Wet squelches joined the moans and groans. Many of the diseased existed as animated wounds. The heavy, phlegmy death rattle and click of snapping teeth added percussion to the low-level hum of suffering.

It took all of Rhys' energy to hold his gasp in when Oscar yanked him back. "What are you *doing*?" he said. "Are you trying to get them to notice you or something?"

So far back now that he couldn't see them and they couldn't see him, Rhys said, "I was just watching them. They're not mad like they have been every other time I've bumped into them. Do you think the effects of the virus are wearing off?"

A sharp shake of his head and Oscar laughed without humour. "*No*, of course they're not. They just haven't seen us yet," he raised an eyebrow at Rhys, "although if you keep on trying to give us away like you are…"

Heat rushed to Rhys' cheeks and he looked down. Oscar may have been a prick, but Rhys had no defence for his actions. He could have given them away just because of his curiosity.

"What goes through your head, Rhys?"

"Don't talk to me like I'm a fucking *child*."

"Stop behaving like one then."

"Whatever," Rhys said. Before the big man could reply, he added, "Anyway, it's not like I'm giving us away. They obviously know we're in the shop. Why would they be gathered around outside if they didn't?"

"Of course they know we're in here, but that's no reason to confirm it by showing them. If they don't see something to get wound up about then they won't get wound up, will they?"

"Okay," Rhys said, "so if you know so much about them, what do we do now?"

"How the fuck am I supposed to know? Your new girlfriend knew a lot of shit about the diseased. What would Vicky do?"

The comment caught Rhys off guard. He watched Oscar through narrowed eyes and studied his features for his reaction. "I've not told you her name yet."

The moment of uncertainty Rhys had seen with the whole Adam / Alan incident didn't present itself like he'd expected it to. "You've said it about ten times already. She's *all* you talk about. I have a good memory for names." A playful smile and he shook his head. "*Clearly* much better than yours."

The signs may have been less obvious this time, but Rhys *hadn't* mentioned Vicky by name. It had been a conscious choice; the less he told the big man, the better.

But Oscar didn't budge and regarded Rhys with his cool and unwavering glare.

There didn't seem to be any point in pursuing the matter. Neither man would budge. Oscar had the fighting skills to help get Rhys to The Alpha Tower. After that, they could go their separate ways and be done with it.

In the silence, an idea hit Rhys and he held a finger in the air. "Wait there."

He walked over to the card reader and swiped his card through it. The red light turned green and he pulled the door open. The hinges groaned again. As he ran down the stairs that represented bike cogs, he listened to Oscar catch the door before it closed.

The big man called down the stairs, "Are you trying to leave me up here or something?"

Rhys stopped and looked up at the man. "No, why?"

"If this door closes, it needs a card to open it from the outside. I'm guessing you still have the card?"

Of course Rhys did. "I'm going to get some of the bigger fireworks—the ones that wouldn't fit in our backpacks; I think we can use them."

Oscar stared at Rhys for a moment before he dipped a slight nod. "Okay. I'll keep the door open while you bring them up."

A nod back and Rhys continued down the stairs. The big man wouldn't be easy to shake should he want to lose him. Rhys dismissed the thought and ran over to the handlebar display case. The glass door to the firework cabinet hung open from when they'd filled their backpacks earlier. When Rhys pulled the tray out, his heart raced as he stared at the huge rockets. They were about to make a lot of fucking noise. He then leaned forward and scooped them up.

~

WITH SO MANY ROCKETS IN HIS ARMS, RHYS NEARLY DROPPED them as he walked up the stairs. He looked up at Oscar, who remained in the doorway staring down at him. A half smile lifted Oscar's face as he took obvious pleasure in Rhys' struggle.

Once Rhys reached the top of the stairs, Oscar remained in the doorway so Rhys had to pause until he got out of his way. When Oscar stepped aside, Rhys walked out onto the roof and squinted as the bright setting sun stung his eyes. Whatever game Oscar wanted to play, he could play it by himself; Rhys didn't have time for his bullshit.

Oscar regarded him with his usual disdain. "So what are you going to do with them? And why didn't you use the ones in your backpack?"

"Because I might need those for later. These are the ones we can't take with us."

The wooden poles attached to the fireworks clattered against the roof when Rhys put them down. His pulse spiked and he dropped into a crouch. The movement tore at his tired leg muscles, but better that than the fuckers below see them.

With Oscar crouched by his side, too, the pair listened to the diseased down below. No worse than usual, the monsters obviously hadn't twigged as to where Rhys and Oscar were yet.

A glance at Oscar, and Rhys' heart stopped for a second. Ice ran down his back when he saw a patch of blood had seeped through Oscar's blue jeans from his right thigh. No wonder he ran with a limp.

When Rhys looked back at Oscar, the big man glared at him. Rhys closed his mouth, took a breath to speak, but said nothing. *Had Oscar been bitten?*

Rhys turned away from Oscar and picked up the firework

he wanted to use. He then stood up and peered at the horde below. None of them looked up.

While on tiptoes, Rhys walked to the edge of the roof, and the stones crunched beneath his feet.

When he got close enough to both see the mob directly beneath him and for the mob to be able see him, he held his breath and retrieved one of the large plant pots from the edge of the roof. Fuck knows what had grown from it. Whatever it had been, it had long since died. If they'd have had more time, the pots may have served as good projectiles at some point. However, with only three and a half hours left before the entire city went up in flames, they'd need a bigger plan. With a few heavy plant pots and stones as ammunition, they'd be there until the middle of next week.

Rhys grunted as he lifted the heavy pot, still full of earth, and his exhausted arms shook from the effort. As he returned to Oscar with it, he made more noise than at any other point up on the roof.

A vent protruded from the roof by about ten centimetres. Rhys leaned the plant pot against it so the top of it angled out over the crowd.

When he took one of the smaller rockets and stuck it into the earth, Oscar laughed. "Are you out of your gourd? That's never going to work."

Rhys didn't respond and his eyes dropped to Oscar's thigh for a moment. The bloodstain had grown to the size of a dinner plate.

Rhys then hunched down, removed a lighter from his pocket, and lit the fuse.

The touch paper hissed and Rhys' mouth dried as he waited what felt like the longest few seconds of his life.

The firework took off with a *whoosh* and screamed as it flew a large arc away from them through the air. It left a red trail behind as it sailed between two towers on the other side of the street.

After it had vanished out of sight, Rhys waited.

Nothing.

"Well, *that* was worth it," Oscar said. "Good job we have you with us. Fucking hell, Einstein, what do you—?"

Before he could finish, a loud bang echoed through the relatively still city. Cries went up from the mob below and the sounds of a stampede ran away from them.

The mature thing would have been to play it cool. Instead, Rhys threw a tight-lipped and smug smile at Oscar. "See, I *told* you it would work."

Oscar walked across the roof and peered down. When he came back to Rhys, he shook his head. "You moved a quarter of them at best."

Rhys pointed at the other rockets in the pile. "What do you think those are for?"

Before Oscar responded, Rhys hunched down again and jabbed the rockets—two at a time—into the flowerpot.

It took about a minute before he had every rocket angled in the same direction.

Oscar stood by with his hands on his hips and watched Rhys with a sneer the entire time. The atmosphere between the two had been icy before Rhys called him out about Vicky. Now that Rhys had as good as called him a liar and openly stared at his wound, bite, or whatever the fuck it was, it had turned positively Arctic.

Rhys knew just two things about the man: he could fight and he couldn't be trusted. Rhys needed someone who could fight, but what did Oscar need from Rhys? Maybe he'd be his first meal when the disease turned him.

Another look at the bloody patch on Oscar's thigh, and Rhys said, "I need you to stay up here."

"What the fuck?"

"You stay up here and light the fireworks. I'll go downstairs and get the bikes ready. Once the diseased have left, I'll open the shutters and we can get out of here."

"So I just let you lock me up on this roof while you go downstairs?"

Rhys walked across to the edge of the roof again and retrieved another ratty plant pot. He grunted from the weight of it and carried it to the door. After he'd swiped the card reader, he pulled the door wide and used the pot to wedge it open. "Better?"

Oscar grunted.

After a quick scan of the rockets in the pot, Rhys said, "We have nine fireworks to set off. After you've set off seven, I'll open the shutters so we're ready to go."

Oscar didn't reply. Instead, he stared at Rhys and his eyes narrowed. The pause lasted for a good ten seconds before he finally nodded. His voice took on a new level of calm that turned the skin on Rhys' arms to gooseflesh. "I swear to you, Rhys, if you fuck me over, I'm going to hunt you down and break your fucking spine. You got that?"

The sooner they got to The Alpha Tower, released the shutters, and parted company, the better. Rhys spun on his heel and headed downstairs.

CHAPTER 11

The tension left Rhys' body the second he descended the stairs. The short time he'd spent up there with Oscar had wound him tighter than a coiled spring. Whatever the man's agenda, just being around him increased the weight of the anxious lump in Rhys' gut. Not only did he have to keep his eyes peeled for the diseased, but he had to watch for the knife that could be firmly wedged into his back at any point.

As he walked down the stairs to the main shop floor, Rhys took a deep breath. The smell of rubber helped clear the stink of rot that had lodged firmly in his sinuses. It felt like the stench would never leave him.

Rhys focused on the closed shutter and walked toward it on tiptoes. When he got just a few metres away, he heard the sound of the diseased on the other side. If they tried, the sheer weight of their collective pressure could force the shutter into the shop. Maybe they hadn't pushed because they didn't know Rhys and Oscar hid inside.

The small respite the scent of rubber provided vanished as Rhys moved closer forward. The sharp tang of rancid meat, excrement, and vomit nearly brought tears to his eyes.

Rhys flinched at the coldness of the shutter when he pressed his face against it to listen. Just centimetres between him and the undead, he heard their phlegmy death rattle again.

When he found a gap in the shutter that he'd missed before, he closed one eye and peered through it. Staring back was an open six-inch gash down the side of one of the diseased's faces that glistened with infection. The shock from the image kicked him square in the face and he stumbled backwards. When he looked behind, he saw he'd stopped just short of crashing into the bike rack in the centre of the shop. His heart pounded as he released a long stream of air from his puffed cheeks. With his hand on his heart, he stared at the shutters and took deep breaths.

The *whoosh* of the first firework cut through his panic. With a hand still on his chest, Rhys' heart galloped against his palm. Several more fireworks shot through the air; some of them released a piercing scream, some of them whooshed like the first. Five in total. Four more to go.

A gulp did nothing to banish the dryness from Rhys' throat—not long before he'd have to take action.

He stepped forward and pressed his ear against the cold shutter. After a series of loud bangs from three of the fireworks that exploded, the breaths of the diseased got heavier.

The last two fireworks exploded and echoed through the city. Enraged screams responded. At first, it came from the diseased far away, but it soon spread through the crowd until the ones directly outside the shop yelled and shrieked with the rest of them.

Rhys closed one eye and peered through the gap again. The diseased with the dark-red, festering wound hadn't moved. Like with the woman earlier, the deep cut had a yellow tinge of pus to it. The thing then shifted to the side and Rhys saw beyond it. Many of the other diseased ran after the fireworks. Thank god, their plan had started to work. At this rate, the space outside the shop would clear quickly.

Another firework shot from the roof and through the gap between the two towers opposite followed by another bang that stirred up more screams. The mass movement disturbed the smell of the diseased and it damn near gassed Rhys. As he waited for the crowd to clear, saliva rained down his throat and he fought against the desire to vomit.

One more firework and he'd lift the shutter.

Although only a few metres away, Rhys wheeled his bike even closer to the shop's exit. He left Oscar's where it was.

A quick glance at the cog stairs and Rhys turned back to the front of the shop. Maybe this should be the end of the road. Sure, Oscar could fight, but that made him even more of a threat to Rhys. At some point, he could turn it on him. The guy seemed pretty fucking volatile, and if it kicked off, he'd beat the shit out of Rhys in a heartbeat. Then there was the cut on his thigh… why had Oscar felt he needed to hide it?

Another peek through the gap in the shutter and Rhys saw the diseased with the wound in its cheek had completely gotten out of the way. Just a few stragglers at the back followed the others down a tight alleyway to the next street over. *It had worked! It had fucking worked.*

Rhys couldn't stop the shake in his hand when he removed the card from his top pocket. He held it near the card reader and listened to the seventh firework *whoosh* through the air. A swipe through the reader, and the light turned from red to green. The mechanism in the door whirred to life and clicked as it lifted the shutter from the ground.

The concrete hurt Rhys' knees when he dropped down onto it. Like the shutters, it had the sting of cold when Rhys pressed his face against it and peered beneath.

As one, what remained of the mob watched the seventh firework fizz through the sky. Like children, they seemed mesmerised by it and doubled their clumsy, shuffled effort to get to where it landed.

Pressed so low down made it impossible to ignore the brown sludge left behind by the crowd. Wherever they went, they excreted a rancid slug trail of gunk. Their wounds seeped constantly, and what they left behind stank worse than anything Rhys had ever smelled. It stank like curdled milk mixed with sewage—it turned his stomach upside down.

When the shutter had lifted high enough, Rhys wheeled his bike out. The gentle tick as the wheels turned filled the near silence left by the abandonment of the diseased.

One final glance back into the shop, and Rhys looked at the cog stairs again. He spoke beneath his breath as he swiped his card through the reader on the outside and the shutter closed. "Sorry, Oscar, but I just don't fucking trust you. You're a liability, mate."

CHAPTER 12

R hys' legs still burned as his muscles strained to match his desire to get away. Despite the reluctance that gripped his exhausted limbs, riding a bike sure beat running. Careful to avoid the large—and what looked like slippery—patches of blood, he weaved and swerved through the streets on his mountain bike. Oscar had pulled away from him, as usual, but Rhys kept a steady pace and remained focused on his deep breaths.

Rhys had gone back for Oscar. He'd gotten no more than about fifty metres from the shop before he turned back around. He couldn't leave him there to perish. If the wound on his leg had been a bite, the man would have turned already. Besides, the lunatic would have found a way out and would have hunted Rhys down like a hound on a scent. No doubt, Oscar would have seen Rhys when he came down-stairs before the shutter had fully closed. He didn't need that kind of fury on his tail, not on top of everything else in the crazy city. Besides, injured or not, Oscar could fight like nobody Rhys had ever met before. Rhys needed that brutality by his side if he were to get to The Alpha Tower.

Now they could move faster, the pair travelled with less caution and shot out of the next alleyway. Two diseased milled about in the street, and before they'd even considered giving chase, Rhys and Oscar had a fifty-metre lead on them. Although the creatures yelled and their clumsy gait hammered a rapid—yet irregular—beat against the ground, the sound of them grew more distant by the second.

Oscar ducked into another alleyway and Rhys followed. The click of the bikes' turning cogs echoed in the tight space.

The sound of the diseased had gone by the time they'd exited the next alley.

After a glance behind, Oscar slowed down and Rhys pulled up next to him. He still panted like an old asthmatic without an inhaler, but at least the ease of riding a bike allowed him to move while he rested.

"I really thought you were going to leave me when I saw you ride out of the shop," Oscar said.

Using the chance to look at their surroundings—and anywhere but at Oscar—Rhys cleared his throat and took several deep breaths. "I told you, there were some stragglers. If I had left the shutter open, you would have come down-stairs to a shop full of the fuckers. I needed to lead them away."

As Rhys looked around, his face flushed hot. Oscar stared at him, and although Rhys saw him do it in his peripheral vision, he kept his eyes on the road ahead. He'd never been a good liar, especially not when under the scrutiny of Oscar's cold glare.

The silence had lasted for a short while before Oscar said, "It didn't look like that."

"Well, it clearly *was* like that," Rhys said. His pulse quickened when he added, "Otherwise you'd still be on the roof waiting for someone to rescue you."

"Or I'd have jumped off and *hunted* you down."

A look across at Oscar's bloody thigh, and Rhys changed the subject. "What happened?"

"Huh?"

"To your thigh? You're bleeding. What happened to it?"

Oscar didn't reply for a moment. He then said, "I ran into some exposed metal."

"So you haven't been—"

"Bitten?" Oscar said. "No. If I'd have been bitten, don't you think I would have turned by now? The wound's bad and it makes it hard for me to move freely, but it isn't a bite."

"So you need me around to help you fight the diseased?"

"*Need*? Don't get too fucking cocky. I think I do more for you than you do for me."

Despite the abrasive response, Rhys saw the truth of it. Oscar felt vulnerable with his leg and needed someone to watch his back.

"Besides," Oscar said, "I may be injured, but I can still outrun *you*."

When Building Seventy-two came into view, Rhys pointed at it. "There it is; that's the building Larissa's in."

Before Oscar had a chance to respond, Rhys sped up and Oscar followed.

WHEN THEY ARRIVED AT THE TOWER, RHYS GOT OFF HIS BIKE and propped it up against one of the brushed steel shutters. The entranceway looked exactly the same as the one Oscar had been trapped in when they first met. Of course it did, every building looked the same except for The Alpha Tower.

The black tiled floor and slight alcove led up to the front

door of the building. Everything else had been wrapped in the protective embrace provided by the shutters.

Despite how much everything had changed, the familiar buzz of anxiety ran through Rhys' gut; a Pavlovian response to a life he'd always hated. Even when hell had risen up onto the streets, the thought of the slow death in his tiny cubicle filled him with dread.

A glance around revealed nothing—no diseased, no anything. They'd been there though; the streets evidenced it clearly: bloodstains, lumps of flesh… even a small arm lay on the floor, but no diseased.

Although he got off his bike too, Oscar remained out in front of the building, his axe raised as he kept watch.

A deep boom rang out when Rhys knocked on the shutters. The hard barrier stung his knuckles.

"Do you wanna make any more fucking noise?" Oscar hissed at him, the enclosed space making his voice echo.

Before Rhys could answer, the enraged scream of the diseased called out. Oscar's eyes widened and he spun around. With his axe raised and ready to strike, he looked up and down the road.

Rhys also lifted his weapon and waited. It sounded like just a couple of diseased, but he needed to be ready should Oscar want backup.

Suddenly two diseased appeared and Rhys jumped backwards. In a flash, Oscar had buried the head of his axe into the skull of one of them, and before it hit the ground, he'd removed it and taken the next one down.

He panted as he loomed over the two bodies and held his right leg in a way that showed his discomfort. Then he turned to Rhys and scowled. "Now fucking hurry up and keep the fucking *noise* down, yeah?"

The first knock on the shutter had done nothing, so Rhys

stepped closer. He found a gap between two of the steel plates and pressed his face into it. He jumped back instantly. Unlike the food pod, several faces stared back at him rather than a solitary eyeball. Their mouths moved, but the thick glass barrier between them made it impossible to hear what they said.

Rhys looked at the thick end of his baseball bat and the gap between the shutters. It looked just about wide enough. The screech of metal against metal set Rhys' teeth on edge, but he persevered and pushed the bat farther into the gap. The tight pinch scratched both the writing and the dried blood from the end of the bat.

The bat made contact with the glass with a slight *ting*. Rhys had enough space to tilt the bat at an angle. Like moving an oar, he used the leverage he'd created to push the head of the bat against the large window.

A glance at Oscar showed the big man continued to watch the street. Good job, really. If he saw what Rhys was about to do, he'd go nuts.

With extra pressure, the window on the other side creaked and moaned and Rhys held his breath. He then bit down on his bottom lip and pulled a little harder just as Oscar said, "*What* the fuck are you..." the glass on the other side popped and whooshed as most of it fell to the floor.

For a moment, Rhys froze and looked at the enraged Oscar. Then the voices of those inside the tower rang out.

"Help us."

"Please get us out of here."

"Please."

Rhys' heart beat on the edge of a panic attack. He jumped forward and hissed through the gap, "Be quiet. Keep the fucking noise down."

No one listened. If anything, their cries for help grew louder.

"If you don't keep the volume down, I'm going to leave you here to rot. I'm trying to help you, but you're *not* making it easy. There's a lot of shit going on out here and the noisier you are, the less chance we all have of surviving this."

Rhys heard three wet crunches and turned around to see three more diseased sporting brain-killing head wounds. Oscar kept his large back to Rhys and focused on the street beyond the tower. He used the t-shirt from one of the diseased to wipe the blood from his axe. Good job Rhys didn't leave him at the shop. Liar or not, he needed him.

A woman's voice came at Rhys through the gap, "What's going on?"

It sounded like Janice, the receptionist. She'd always been the mother hen, the one to get involved in everyone else's business. "Janice, it's Rhys. Can you please get Larissa and I'll explain everything."

"What's going on, Rhys?"

"Just get Larissa, yeah? I don't have time to repeat myself."

"You don't have time?! We've been trapped in here for hours, you *owe* us an explanation."

Rhys bounced on the balls of his feet and tapped his baseball bat to keep his impatience at bay. He looked at Oscar who shook his head. A deep breath and he said, "Janice, *please* get Larissa."

"Don't you talk to me like that; I'm not going anywhere until—"

"Look, you stupid bitch, if you take much more fucking time, I won't be able to get you out of this building at all because I'll be *dead*. Now get Larissa before my fucking time runs out, yeah?"

A heavy sigh and the click of Janice's high heels marched away from the door.

IT COULDN'T HAVE TAKEN ANY MORE THAN A MINUTE, BUT for Rhys it felt like an age. Left in the open, vulnerable to an onslaught, he paced and twitched until he finally heard Larissa's voice.

"I'm here, Rhys."

Another scream came from behind them. Although Rhys couldn't see where they were, he checked Oscar, who continued to keep lookout. On high alert, he had his axe raised and scanned the area. He obviously hadn't seen anything yet either.

"Larissa, are you okay?"

Although she offered a meek reply, she still said, "Yeah, I'm fine. It's getting pretty crazy in here though. The water's out and it's hot. It's ratcheting up the tension and people are turning on one another. What's going on out there?"

"It ain't pretty. There are zombies out here."

"*What*?"

"I know… it sounds crazy, but there are real-life, honest-to-god zombies out here. But they're worse than the movie zombies."

"Worse?"

"It's fucking mental. Look, I've found a way to get the shutter raised on the buildings, but I needed to come and tell you first. When these shutters lift, you need to run for all you're worth and get the fuck away from this city as quickly as possible. I have Flynn."

"He's out there with you?"

"No, I've left him with someone."

"You've *what*?"

A glance at the Superman watch, and Rhys said, "In just over three hours, this city is going to go up in a ball of flames. It's been set to incinerate everything; I'm guessing to kill off the virus that made the zombies. I couldn't bring Flynn back into the city with me because I need to get in and out before the place burns. He'd only slow me down. I'm here because he wants his mummy. I couldn't walk away and let this city burn with you in it. A boy needs his mum. The main thing is, he's in safe hands, trust me."

Larissa didn't reply, and when Rhys looked over, he caught Oscar as he glared at him.

Rhys shook his head and returned his attention to the gap between the shutters. "When these barriers lift, I need you to head for Central Station. I'm going to get Dave to meet me there too. From there, we'll get out of the city together, okay?"

Her voice wavered. "Okay."

"If anything happens and you can't get to Central Station, meet me at the drawbridge at eight forty-five. This place will go up at nine."

Another scream—closer this time—and Oscar called over his shoulder, "We need to leave *now*, Rhys." Oscar lifted his bike from the ground and straddled it. "Come on."

"Who's that?" Larissa asked.

"It doesn't matter."

"What if I can't get to the drawbridge?"

Rhys backed away from the shutter. "You have to. If you don't, you're dead."

Her words trembled when she said, "Please don't let me die. I love you. I've always loved you and I want you back. We can be a happy family again."

When Clive said, "Hey, what about us?" Rhys shook his

head; the poor guy must have been there the entire time. At least he now understood what a ruthless bitch she was. Thank god Rhys didn't have to deal with that any more.

Rhys jumped onto his bike, but before he could ride out of the entranceway, a line of diseased tore across in front of him and stopped. They barred his way like a police blockade.

As one, they stood and stared at him through bloody eyes. They breathed heavily and swayed on the spot. They looked like they could fall over at any moment, like the only thing that kept them on their feet was the desire to destroy whatever stood in front of them.

Unable to prevent the shake in his limbs, Rhys watched them snap their teeth as their mouths twisted into grotesque snarls and blood ran down their chins.

When Rhys looked past them, he couldn't see Oscar. A dry gulp and his breath ran away with him. "Shit."

CHAPTER 13

Time seemed to pause as the line of diseased stared at Rhys.
Their usual impatience to get at their prey had momentarily abandoned them. It was as if they knew they had the upper
hand, and although their expression remained the same—hateful,
dark, and hungry—something about the way they stood there
suggested they savoured the moment. Like they knew he'd
escaped them too many times already. He'd run out of lives.

With his bike between his legs, Rhys wound his baseball
bat back and wrung the grip. Sweat turned his palms slick and
his heart fluttered as he waited for them to make the first
move. Whatever happened, they would have to fight hard to
take him down.

The creatures snarled and moaned. They rocked from side
to side, but none of them moved toward him.

Then Larissa spoke, "Rhys, what's happening? What's
going on out there?"

Her voice broke their focus. As one, the diseased looked
past Rhys at the small gap between the armoured plates.

"Rhys?"

Rhys held his breath and watched the diseased as he slipped his bat between his rucksack and his back. The metal weapon pushed painfully against his spine so he wriggled from side to side to ease his discomfort. He gripped the bike's rubber handles. If he rode directly at them, he may get out of there. Whatever happened, he couldn't stand toe to toe with six of them.

When he wheeled the bike pedal back slowly, Rhys tensed up at each click the cog made. Any disturbance to the delicate balance could give his intentions away and trigger the inevitable rush forward. He placed his foot on the now raised pedal and continued to stare. His tired eyes stung from his refusal to blink.

Suddenly a *whoosh* and a loud *wheee* sounded out and Rhys' heart leapt into his throat. Yellow sparks flew toward him and the firework scored a direct hit into the back of one of the diseased. It caught in its clothes, and the thing spun around as the projectile fizzed and kicked out smoke and sparks.

Rhys winced in anticipation of the loud—

Bang!

The sound echoed off every wall in the alcove entrance-way. Rhys' ears rang and his head spun.

Rhys shook the dizziness off and refocused. Fire chewed into the clothes of the diseased who still had a part of the fire-work attached to it, and the others backed away, causing a gap to open up in their ranks.

Rhys rode straight at the space.

A hand caught his shoulder on his way through. The contact wobbled him, but he kept his balance. Another rocket shot past him. It flew so close to the side of his head it blew his hair back. It crashed into the shutters at the front of

Building Seventy-two. The diseased screamed before it exploded with another loud bang.

Rhys headed straight for Oscar, and then shot past him. Oscar turned his bike to follow him. The diseased may have been fast, but they wouldn't be able to catch the pair.

The road seemed clear. Several alleyways on Rhys and Oscar's left led to Dave's building, each of them as unoccupied as the next. Rhys had to choose one so he turned down the next he came to. He didn't need to look behind to realise Oscar had caught up with him. The close sound of the big man's heavy breaths and the ticking of his bike in motion told Rhys everything he needed to know—despite a bad leg, Oscar fucking owned him.

With no diseased in front of him and the end of the alleyway in sight, Rhys glanced behind. The diseased Oscar had fired at had only just entered the alley with their usual clumsiness. They crashed into the walls as they ran.

The alleyway opened up into another wide road. The low sun blinded Rhys as he turned toward Building Twenty-one.

Another glance behind and Rhys saw Oscar shoot out of the alley a second later.

When Rhys turned back around to look in front, everything shifted into slow motion. He saw it a second before it happened but had no control to change the sequence of events. First, the front tyre of his bike hit one of the large metal poles in the middle of the road. It felt like everything sank into it on impact, as if the bike buckled the second it made contact. The back of the bike lifted from the ground and propelled Rhys forward. His arms windmilled as he sailed through the air. He put his hands out in front of him and hit the concrete hard. A jolt ran up him that kicked a sharp pain through both shoulder blades and across his back.

The clatter of his baseball bat bounced away from him, and Rhys slid along on his front.

He looked up in time to see Oscar shoot past. Numb from the collision, Rhys jumped to his feet. The pain would come, but only once the adrenaline had died down. He looked first at Oscar's back, and then at the alleyway they'd just exited. Screams shot out of it into the street.

A violent flutter took a hold of Rhys' heart as he stood there and looked at his bike. The impact had bent the front wheel to an almost right angle. He pulled his hair away from his eyes as he exhaled hard and the screams grew louder.

CHAPTER 14

Paralysed with fear, Rhys stood and stared at his bike. His brain said 'run', but his legs hadn't got the message. The numb ache of future pain twisted from the base of his spine to the top of his neck. At present, it thrummed as a dull throb, but it would hurt... Boy, would it hurt.

The thunder of clumsy feet hammered up the alleyway. Their phlegmy breaths called out amidst the several that screamed. Rhys remained rooted to the spot.

Then Oscar shot back past him toward the alley. "Oscar?"

The big man threw his bike from side to side from the effort of cycling and shouted over his shoulder, "*Run, you fucking fool! I'll distract them.*"

Rhys sprung to life, retrieved his baseball bat, and turned to see the first of the diseased emerge from the alley as Oscar rode past it. They gave chase; they never even looked Rhys' way. Guilt weighed heavy on Rhys' heart. Maybe he'd got Oscar all wrong. Not only had he just saved his life, but he'd done it in spite of the fact that Rhys as good as left him for dead at the bike shop. He'd been such a dick to do that.

With the closest alley just metres away, Rhys darted down

it before any of the diseased saw him.

THE ALPHA TOWER STOOD PROMINENT ON THE HORIZON AS the only tower in the city without shutters around it. However, before he went there, Rhys had to see Dave. Like Larissa, Dave needed to know exactly what to do when the shutters lifted.

No doubt, Oscar would head to The Alpha Tower; Rhys could meet him there afterwards.

The only difference between the pedestrianized areas and the roads were the lack of poles that protruded from the ground. Just as wide and straight, they could be driven down quite easily if they didn't all lead to a dead-end. They could only be accessed via alleyways.

The noise of the diseased ran a perpetual murmur in the background, a constant groan of discomfort and dissatisfaction. It came from every angle, almost as if the buildings were infected too. It ran so rife it had become a part of the fabric of the city. Rhys could deal with the sounds in the background. *Long may they remain there.*

As if on cue, the rasp of a diseased shot across the otherwise abandoned area. Although he couldn't yet see the monster, by the sound of its phlegmy death rattle, he had seconds to get the fuck out of the way.

With the closest tower just metres away, Rhys ducked into the recessed entrance and lifted his bat. His pulse kicked to the point where it unsettled his breath and his head spun. A mixture of exhaustion, dull pain, and adrenaline made him tremble where he stood.

The scrape of the creature's clumsy feet drew closer and Rhys pressed his back into the steel shutter in the tower's entranceway. Despite the lowered temperature outside, the hot metal retained the day's heat.

The sound of the diseased got louder and Rhys watched the space he expected it to fill.

Then two of them appeared. They walked down the middle of the pedestrianized area, their uncoordinated shuffle a stumble away from sending them sprawling. Their docile state stood in stark contrast to the fury-driven monsters on the tail of a scent.

The smell of the diseased wafted Rhys' way, so rich it made his eyes water. He fought back his retch.

He continued to shake as he watched them pass. It was a man and a woman, not that gender mattered to them anymore. The bite mark in the man's cheek ran so deep that Rhys saw a white flash of bone beneath it. He couldn't see how the woman had turned. Maybe a hideous gash ran down the other side of her face, or a huge tear in her flesh that revealed most of her skull beneath.

They could have looked over and seen Rhys at any moment, but they didn't. Listless and damaged, they shuffled along without a glance his way, their focus ahead of them and jaws hung loose.

When they left Rhys' sight, he released a heavy sigh.

Then he waited to give them time to move on before he stepped out into the street again.

AFTER A FEW MINUTES, RHYS CHECKED FLYNN'S SUPERMAN watch. Twenty minutes since he'd last looked; in less than three hours the accursed island, and everything on it, would be burned to a crisp.

Rhys wriggled the walkie-talkie free from his trouser

pocket and turned it over to inspect it. It seemed to have survived the crash intact. After a quick check that the volume remained low, Rhys flicked it on to call Vicky.

She answered almost instantly. "Hello?"

"Hi, how are things?"

"We're all good. You?"

A deep breath and Rhys said, "I'm hanging on. I've met a person who also wants to rescue somebody, so we've teamed up. We're keeping each other alive, although there's something I don't trust about him."

"Oh?"

"He knew your name."

Vicky's reply snapped back. "My name?"

"Yeah. I'm sure I didn't tell it to him, but he knew it all the same."

The sharpness left her tone. "W… what's his name?"

"Oscar. At least that's what he told me it is. The fella's handy in a fight though. He's saved my arse on more than one occasion already. I'd be dead by now if it wasn't for him."

Silence.

"Vicky?"

"Yeah… sorry; I'm worried about you, Rhys."

"Don't be; I'm fine. Can I talk to Flynn?"

The small voice of his son came out of the speaker. "Hi, Dad."

Rhys' eyes burned with tears and he started to tremble. He cleared the lump from his throat. "Are you okay, mate?"

"I'm fine. When are you coming back? Have you found Mummy?"

"I won't be long now. I've spoken to Mummy and she's going to be coming out of the city with me. Just hang on there, yeah?"

"Okay, Dad."

"I love you, mate."

"I love you too, Dad."

By the time Vicky came back on, tears ran down Rhys' cheeks.

"Just be careful, yeah?" she said. She still sounded distant; knowing that Oscar used her name had clearly unsettled her. Before Rhys could say anything, she said, "I'll see you before nine."

Rhys nodded for a few seconds before he cleared his throat again. It did little to take the warble from his voice. "See you then." He flicked the walkie-talkie off and took a deep breath.

Rhys then poked his head out and saw the place looked clear. A couple of cautious steps later gave him a better view of the pedestrianized area; the diseased had gone for now.

Before anything else could come, he crossed the street. With the slightest twist at the base of his back, he ran awkwardly like a lizard over hot sand, before he disappeared down yet another alleyway.

Prior to the lockdown, the city had been so light Rhys never noticed the tightness of the walkways. Now the reflective windows had been covered, half the city became a shadowy maze.

The constant moan of torment that rode on the back of the breeze didn't help the mood either. Summit City had turned from a shining bastion of commerce into a gloomy, hellish, labyrinthine nightmare.

When Rhys came to the end of the next alley, he poked his head out and saw Dave's tower. His heart sank. Thick clouds of black smoke squeezed through the armoured shell and rose into the sky like an ominous flare. Instead of asking for help and attention, it seemed to mark the building as a place that had been lost.

CHAPTER 15

When Rhys got to within ten metres of Dave's tower, the smoke hung so thick in the air that every inhalation stimulated a rasping cough. Each deep bark not only called out to any diseased in the area, but also threw stars across his vision and made his head spin.

Anyone other than Dave, and Rhys would have written them off as dead; everyone in the tower had surely been killed by now. With The Alpha Tower so close and time running out, he would have made a beeline straight for that but he owed it to his best mate. He couldn't write him off before he'd checked to be certain.

Rhys pulled his hand inside his shirtsleeve and clamped it across his mouth. The thick fabric did little to filter the smoke and he found it nearly impossible to breathe through. He freed his hand and used that to breathe through instead. God knows if it helped or not.

No matter how many times Rhys blinked, the thick smoke burned his eyes, and tears streamed down his cheeks.

He only found the shutter at the front when he crashed into it. It felt warm to touch. With so much smoke around the building, it must have been the fire rather than the sun that heated it.

Like on Building Seventy-two, it had the same gap between the sheets of steel. Smoke poured through the gap.

Rhys looked around and saw nothing. Even if his eyes had remained clear, the dense and noxious cloud would have prevented him seeing any farther than a few feet.

The crackle and roar of the fire inside the building drowned out everything else; even the call of the diseased.

After a deep breath, Rhys pushed his face into the gap. The glass had already been smashed and the smoke burned his eyes worse than before. It felt like he'd poured detergent into them.

Rhys pulled away, rested his hands on his knees, and coughed to the point where he heaved.

Several gulps cleared the taste of plastic, and after pulling in another breath, he pushed his face into the gap again. He spoke on the exhale. "Hello," and then turned away so he could press his ear to the gap and breathe more freely.

No one answered. *Of course they didn't fucking answer. Everyone had died in there.*

One more try for Dave's sake.

Another deep breath, several body-flipping coughs, and he called again, "Hello! Is there anyone there?"

A pair of bloodshot eyes appeared at the gap and Rhys jumped back. Wild and streaked with tears, they almost looked like they had the disease—almost. They weren't coated with a film of blood.

"Help us," the man said as the eyes widened. "There's not many of us left in here. The smoke and fire has killed so many already." A deep wheeze and he coughed. His voice faded. "Please, help us."

Rhys strained his ears and heard the sobs and cries of a

handful of people behind the man. "Is Dave Martin still in there?"

The person on the other side of the shutter paused for a moment. "Yes, yes he is." He turned away from Rhys. "Dave? This guy's asking to speak to you."

While he waited, Rhys looked behind and rubbed his eyes to try and clear his vision. It didn't help; if the diseased wanted to rush the front of the building now, they'd find an exhausted, gassed, and blinded sitting duck.

When the damp eyes of his best mate appeared, Rhys' lip buckled and grief wedged as a hot lump in his throat. It tightened his words. "Dave? Thank god you're okay."

Dave spoke with a croak in his voice. "I won't be for much longer. You need to get us out of here, brother."

"I will, I promise. What the fuck happened, anyway? This isn't the first building I've found on fire. Is it some kind of electrical fault?"

"Some bright spark thought setting the building on fire would trigger a system to release the shutters."

"Someone did this on *purpose*?"

After a heavy coughing fit, Dave said, "I know. Fucked up, right?"

"Well, I'm going to The Alpha Tower now. They have a room where I can override the defence system. That'll set you free." Rhys stopped to cough. "But you have to be ready to run the second the shutters lift. There are zombies out here. Real-life, crazed, lunatic zombies." Before Dave could say anything else, Rhys continued, his voice strained as his throat tightened. "I ain't shitting you. You just need to trust me, okay?"

After Rhys had coughed again, he listened to Dave say, "Okay."

"So when the shutters come up, run for all you're worth

and get to Central Station. I'll meet you there as soon as I can, and we'll get out of this godforsaken city."

Uncertainty hung on Dave's words. "Okay. Please hurry, Rhys."

Rhys nodded. "Hang on in there, mate. I'll be as quick as I can. I love you, man."

It came out as another feeble croak, but Dave replied. "I love you too."

CHAPTER 16

A lthough he currently saw the world through blurred vision, Rhys ran as fast as he could from Tower Twenty-one. With such poor sight, every step could trip him, but his head spun and he couldn't breathe. He had to get away before he collapsed.

His eyes burned from the smoke damage. Tears moistened his cheeks and he had a thick lump stuck in his throat. Maybe grief played a large part in blinding him. Just the sight of Dave's face... His friend's usual self-assurance had gone, robbed from him by his dire situation. Rhys had never seen him so vulnerable.

A heavy sniff, his sinuses clogged, and he wiped his runny nose with the back of his sleeve. Dave needed him and Rhys would make damn sure he got him out of the tower. If Larissa died so be it; at least he'd tried for his son's sake. But if he lost Dave... it didn't bear thinking about.

Once he was free from the thick smoke, Rhys stopped. He leaned on his knees and coughed at the ground. The heavy barks bucked through his body and aggravated the ache at the base of his spine.

While he fought for breath—the taste of burned plastic at the back of his throat—he stood up straight and looked around. Although his eyes still watered, distance from the smoke made it easier to see. The area seemed free of the diseased.

The alleyway across the street led to the square with The Alpha Tower in it. When Rhys inhaled again, his lungs felt like they had half their capacity, at best.

He glanced at Flynn's Superman watch. Two hours and forty-five minutes until the streets were flooded with fire. Another look up and down the street, and Rhys ran across it.

RHYS PANTED WHEN HE ARRIVED AT THE END OF THE alleyway and looked into the square. He rubbed his face; his tears had driven some of the smoke from his eyes, which helped him to see clearer. The square seemed vacant but looks meant nothing with the city in its current state.

Another couple of deep breaths, and the tightness in his lungs eased. After several more blinks, his misty vision cleared some more. The chaos of just a few hours ago had gone, although the memory remained burned into Rhys' mind in high definition. His heart raced as he looked at the open space.

The lowering sun lit up the square. When they opened the shutters, they'd be unleashing chaos on the city, but at least the shiny windows would return light to some of the dark crevices. If he never ran down a gloomy alley again, it would be too soon.

A final round of forced blinks, and Rhys rubbed his eyes yet again. When his vision cleared, he lost his breath. The vast expanse of concrete that paved the square glistened.

Spilled blood covered what seemed to be every inch of it. The sun reflected off it, the blood deep enough that it hadn't dried yet.

Not only had it painted the pavement red, but blood also coated the stone benches, and several of them had been broken clean in half. It must have taken a serious whack to break them; they looked like they could withstand a lightning bolt. Thank fuck he got out of the square when he did.

Every part of the open space had been stained or damaged by the diseased. Everywhere except The Alpha Tower and— his heart skipped—the fountain. The almost white concrete wall remained immaculate, even in the sea of blood that surrounded it. Jake wasn't in the water anymore either; although how the fuck he went anywhere with broken shins...

The only difference between the fountain in front of Rhys now and the one he'd left earlier that day was the water. The pump worked fine, it recycled the water as it should have. The water itself, however, had been dyed bright red.

Rhys squinted and his eyes ached at the sides from where the smoke had dried his skin. A look back at the ground again and he saw chunks of flesh scattered across it. Some pieces were so big and nondescript they could have been packaged up and served in the chilled section of a supermarket. Others retained their human form. A strip of skin lay to his right; about a foot long, muscle still clung to it. Short, curly hairs ran the entire length of it and Rhys saw the corner of a tattoo. It looked like it had been rent from someone's leg.

Before he could think on it further, the thwapping of a helicopter blade vibrated through his chest and disturbed the air around him.

Rhys pulled back into the alley and watched a large black chopper come in over the top of a couple of towers.

The air forced down from the blades tousled Rhys' hair

and sent ripples over the surface of the layer of blood that coated the square.

The helicopter lowered over the middle of the square and stopped about ten metres from the ground. The loud rotors battered his eardrums, and the wind flapped so violently, Rhys had to blink repeatedly. Two men, dressed from head to toe in black and wearing helmets with tinted visors, lowered a large cage out of it.

After about thirty-seconds, the cage scraped against the concrete ground. The men pulled back into the helicopter and Rhys lost sight of them.

About the size of a small car, the cage remained still. The men had given the chain attached to it enough slack so it didn't shift around with the bird above.

When Rhys cupped his hands around his eyes to protect them from the wind, he finally saw the contents of the cage and his stomach sank. Icy dread drained the strength from his muscles, and he shook where he stood. He could only manage two words. "Fucking hell."

CHAPTER 17

One side of the cage fell away and hit the concrete with a loud *crash*. It created an opening into the rectangular prison. It had clearly been designed as a trap; bait had been tied inside the cage on the far wall. The sound of the loud rotors had drowned him out, but since Rhys had seen him, he couldn't help but hear the naked man's screams. He yelled so loud his voice cracked and wavered. Rhys gulped against the taste of plastic in his own throat as he watched on.

In a matter of seconds, the scream of the diseased joined that of the man. A glance across the square, and Rhys saw the pack. Clumsy in their desire to get at the man, they sprinted straight for the cage. They ran like they always did—heavy footed and right on the edge of their balance. One misstep and they'd crash flat on their faces. Rhys did a quick head-count. Seven... seven diseased—all of them male.

It hadn't seemed possible, but when the man saw them, he screamed louder still. Rhys' sight cleared with every passing second, and he now saw him thrash more violently than before. His exposed penis shook. Lacerations covered his body. Maybe the disease would be a relief from what he'd evidently been through already. At no more than twenty-five, this man's short life had reached a torturous conclusion.

As the diseased closed in on him, their roars grew louder.

The man's screams changed into violent shaking sobs. With his hands, feet, and neck tied to the cage, he fell limp like a hung puppet. Hope had obviously left him.

With an accelerated pulse, Rhys watched on. In a perfect world, he would have done something. They didn't live in a perfect world though, and he had too many people he loved that needed him.

One of the diseased had broken away from the pack. With no more than about ten metres between him and the entrance to the cage, it seemed to speed up.

The man looked at him. His mouth moved but nothing came out, almost like he screamed on a new frequency—a frequency that could only be heard in hell.

When the lead diseased entered the cage, the metal bars rattled as they bounced against the concrete ground. The other diseased entered behind him just as the one in the lead reached the naked man.

Metal clattered; both the diseased and the man screamed, and the rotors turned. Yet all of that paled in significance when Rhys heard the wet crack as two bodies collided.

The man cried out as the lead diseased bit into his face. As if the cage had been electrified, he shook and yelled as it chowed down. Seconds later, the other six crashed into him. Shortly after, his screams fell silent.

A cable that hung down from the helicopter snapped taut and the cage door slammed shut. It trapped the diseased inside the cage with the man—not that they noticed; they shared a single-minded purpose as they all chomped onto a part of the now flaccid corpse.

By the time they'd finished with him, the helicopter had

lifted the cage several metres from the ground. The man had been reduced to a torn up piece of meat. The position of his shackles seemed to be the only thing that retained his human form. Covered in blood to the point where Rhys couldn't see any of his skin, the man looked like he belonged in a butcher's freezer.

Then he twitched and Rhys jumped. His sore throat turned arid. *What the fuck?*

Another twitch and the man lifted his bloody face to stare at the other monsters in the cage. Where he'd been the focus of their interest only moments before, none of them even looked his way now.

Only when the man opened his mouth did Rhys see the orientation of his face. Skinned to the flesh beneath, his head didn't even resemble a skull. It looked more like an overripe piece of fruit, juicy and fleshy beyond any kind of definition. Suddenly he vomited what looked like about a pint of blood.

When he'd finished, he opened one of his eyes. The other seemed to have been gouged out or battered shut. As the cage moved farther away, it became harder for Rhys to see the finer details. *Thank god.*

Another sharp jolt ran through the man and he released a wet roar. The dampness that gargled from his throat sounded like a man drowning.

His slow moment of awakening sped up as the jilted fury of the disease took over. He snapped his jaws and thrashed his head from side to side. Now too far away for Rhys to see anything other than his form, the man shook as if he thought he could break free of his bonds.

The helicopter continued to rise and took the man and his new friends with it. Rhys squinted against the downward wind as he watched on.

Once the helicopter had cleared the top of the buildings, it tilted in the sky and pulled away from the square.

A few seconds later, the thing had disappeared from view.

Rhys glanced at his watch. Only two and a half hours left. Whatever the people in the chopper were doing didn't matter; Rhys had to keep on. At least the helicopter had drawn the diseased in the square out of hiding; hopefully it would be clear for him now.

The Alpha Tower stood shutterless and as indomitable as ever. He focused on his breath, but it did little to combat the tension that twisted his intestines, and his lungs continued to ache from the smoke that came from Dave's tower. He checked around one last time. It looked clear. A nod to himself as he focused on the tower and Rhys ran out into the square.

CHAPTER 18

R hys slipped several times as he sprinted across the open square. Blood covered every inch of the ground, although, from what he could tell, all of the diseased had gone from the area around The Alpha Tower. Not that he could be sure of much in the fucked-up city.

The low sun forced Rhys to squint as he ran.

When he reached the other side of the square, The Alpha Tower blocked the sun's glare and he saw Oscar for the first time. He'd obviously been there all the while and had watched Rhys run toward him. The large man leaned against the wall by the entrance and had propped his bike up next to him. He seemed almost relaxed, like someone waiting for a bus or something equally as trivial.

He'd only get a blank stare from Oscar until they were close enough to speak, so Rhys focused on the tower instead. He'd gotten so close that on a normal day, security would have shooed him away by now.

The Alpha Tower stood as the only skyscraper in the city that hadn't been surrounded by steel shutters. Its white walls and blacked-out windows seemed even more imposing

surrounded by the huge grey pods that had once been government administration offices, and were now prisons.

Rhys looked for signs of smoke and saw none. *Good fucking job.* It would take a lot to persuade him to enter a building on fire. Grief twisted in his chest. He had to hurry for Dave's sake.

When Rhys caught up to Oscar, both his low level of fitness and smoke-impaired lungs prevented him from speaking to the man. His throat stuck when he swallowed, and he continued to gasp for air. He pointed back across the square and finally managed, "Did you just *see* that?"

Oscar stared at him.

"The *helicopter*, Oscar; the huge fucking helicopter with the trap beneath it."

A glint sparkled in Oscar's eyes. "Yeah, fucked up, wasn't it?"

Words abandoned Rhys as he stared at the man. He looked like he knew something Rhys didn't, almost like he got some kind of twisted pleasure from what he'd just witnessed. "What were they doing?"

A sharp shrug and Oscar said, "How the fuck would I know?" He looked around. "I've been standing here like a lemon waiting for you to turn up. I feel like zombie bait. So if you don't mind, how about you open this fucking door and we get into the tower? Or do you want to see how much longer we can tempt fate before our luck runs out?"

The man's directness ran unease straight to Rhys' core. Sure, he'd be desperate to get into the tower too if he'd stood there waiting for that time, but yet again, Oscar's behaviour seemed like a cover for something else. Despite all that Oscar had done for him, something sinister lurked beneath the surface of the man. He didn't trust the fucker one little bit.

Still, Rhys needed Oscar. The Alpha Tower would no

doubt be overflowing with diseased. If Rhys could choose anyone to have his back in a tight spot against them, Oscar came a close second only to Vicky. The guy knew how to fight them without a gun—leg injury or not—and right now, Rhys needed that from a companion more than anything else.

"Are you going to carry on staring at me," Oscar said, "or are you going to open this fucking building? You can take a fucking picture of me for later if it'll make you *hurry up*."

Flynn's Superman watch showed less than two and a half hours left. He looked at The Alpha Tower again and then back at Oscar.

Oscar shrugged. "*Well?*"

Oscar had helped Rhys every time he'd needed it. He had no reason to suspect him of anything untoward.

When Rhys pulled the map Vicky had drawn for him from his top pocket, he turned it around and showed it to Oscar. As he held it open, his hands shook.

"Vicky drew that for you, did she? She's proven to be quite handy in all of this, wouldn't you say?"

And then he goes and says something like that. Without the ability to rewind time, Rhys couldn't know if he'd told Oscar Vicky's name or not. It still jarred him to hear Oscar say it though. Not that it mattered what Oscar knew; the second the shutters came up, these two were done.

Rhys straightened the crinkles from the map as best as he could. The paper rustled in the near silence of the square. "We need to head straight for the elevator; that'll take us to the top floor." Although the map showed just a crude rendering of what they would no doubt find up there, it showed enough. "It looks like we have to head to the very end of the corridor we come out on. There are two rooms at the end." A warble ran through Rhys' voice and it threatened to expose his lie. "The room on the right has the computer to override the shutters."

"And the one on the left?" Oscar said.

The rendered boxes represented the rooms at the end of the corridor and nothing more. Rhys focused on them as heat flushed his cheeks. "I dunno; let's just worry about getting to that back room. I'm guessing it's not important, otherwise Vicky would have said."

Oscar pointed at the room on the right. "Don't we need another clearance card to get into it?"

"Yes. Hopefully there'll be some scientists up there that we can take one from."

"Hopefully?"

"I'm not fucking psychic, Oscar. I'd say there's a good chance, but if I'm being honest, I don't have a fucking clue what we're going to find in this building. We have nothing but a baseball bat and an axe on us. Your leg's fucked and I've inhaled lungfuls of smoke. We could be walking straight into hell."

The glint returned to Oscar's eyes, almost as if the prospect of chaos excited him.

"All I know," Rhys said, "is that I have loved ones who need rescuing." Another check of his watch. "We don't have long before this place goes up like a lit match to petrol. So are you ready, or do you want to spend what little time we have left complaining?"

Oscar locked a penetrative stare on Rhys. The heat returned to Rhys' cheeks. He'd seen Rhys' lie about the rooms at the end. He must have worked it out.

"Right," Rhys said and clapped his hands together. "Let's fucking do this."

The building may have looked different from all of the others in Summit City but the card reader on the outside looked exactly the same. When Rhys swallowed, it hurt, and the taste of molten plastic still sat in his throat. He couldn't smell a thing since he'd left Dave's tower other than smoke. He removed Vicky's card and his hand shook worse than before. He took another deep breath and swiped it through the reader.

The second the red light turned green, Oscar shoved him aside and barged through.

Hopefully he'd believed Rhys. Hopefully he'd go for the room on the right.

CHAPTER 19

The second Rhys stepped into The Alpha Tower, he drew an involuntary breath. Tall and wide, the foyer took up what could have been the first five floors had they chosen to utilise the space. The Alpha Tower seemed to be the only place in the city where efficiency bowed down to beauty.

The floor, as large as a football field, looked like it had been made from one piece of marble. The walls had been made from the same material, and like the floor, Rhys couldn't see the joins. Several grand black leather sofas had been placed on the floor. Everything that could have a trim, had been outlined in gold.

"Talk about luxury," Rhys said. "This place looks more like a swanky hotel than an office building."

Rhys had to squint to see to the other end of the vast room. Two gold doors lay flush with the far wall. They stood side by side, separated by a strip of green marble about a metre wide. Each door had a small round call button next to it and nothing else. Two letters had been inlaid into the marble halfway up the wall. Gold, like every other trim in the foyer, they stood about ten metres high and five metres wide. They read 'AT'.

Like Rhys, Oscar looked around the room. Unlike Rhys—who stood limp jawed with his arms flopped by his side—he had his axe raised, ready for use.

Rhys finally snapped out of it and looked for danger. Another good reason to have Oscar around; the man remained permanently vigilant when Rhys could only gawp like an awestruck child.

Rhys leaned close to Oscar and said, "See anything?"

"No, it looks—"

The roar of the diseased echoed through the cavernous reception area. The shrill call bounced off the hard walls, which made it difficult to pinpoint its origin. Rhys spun on the spot and his heart pounded in his neck. Although he swallowed, his throat remained dry. "Where the fuck did that noise come from?"

The darkness shifted to the left, and six diseased burst from the shadows. The group consisted of four women and two men.

They sprinted on the edge of their balance as if they'd fall face first on their next step. Their arms slashed the air in front of them and they snapped their teeth. The top halves of their bodies leaned forward, but instead of watching the floor, they lifted their faces and glared at the pair through bloody eyes.

Rhys unsheathed his bat from where he'd slid it between his rucksack and his back. He gripped the handle and wound back, ready to swing. In his peripheral vision, he saw Oscar drop into a defensive crouch, his axe still raised.

Some of the diseased ran quicker than the others. The slap of their feet beat against the hard floor as they bore down on Rhys and Oscar.

With the mob closer, Rhys re-counted. *Eight! Four each.* They could cope with that. Just.

The three fastest opened up a clear lead and left the pack behind.

Rhys clenched his jaw, turned his shoulder to face their attackers, and swung at the lead diseased's nose. Its momentum carried it forward, but Rhys' blow threw its top half back. The monster's legs kicked up as its torso hurtled toward the floor, back first. It seemed like it shook the ground from where it hit it so hard.

"Fuck off, cunt," Rhys yelled as he swung for the downed creature. The thing's skull damn near popped from the blow, and a puff of rot and vinegar rushed up and smothered Rhys.

Rhys heaved, drew several heavy breaths, and looked up at Oscar.

Two quick strikes let Oscar drop both of his diseased in quick succession. Both had died before they'd hit the ground. As they lay there, limp and lifeless, their wounds leaked across the marble.

Before he had time to dwell on it, the other five descended on them.

Rhys took three this time. He swung for them one after the other. All three of them fell to the ground. As he rushed over to them, he heard Oscar behind him. The big man's deep grunts followed by a wet squelch for each diseased, and then silence. His mechanical efficiency unsettled Rhys. *What would he be like without an injury?*

Rhys gripped the handle of his bat with both hands and let the thick end hang down as he stood over the first diseased. He drove a sharp jab straight into the centre of its face. When he moved onto the next one, he screamed and forced the end of the aluminium bat down again.

The last kill—a blonde woman no older than about

twenty-five—stared up at him through blood-red eyes. Her mouth worked slowly; the blow had only stunned her. Rhys clenched his jaw and drove the bat straight into her dainty nose.

Out of breath, Rhys stared at Oscar. For the first time since he'd met him, he saw the large man had broken a sweat and breathed heavily too. "You ready to go?" Rhys said.

Oscar nodded.

The pair of them ran across the foyer toward the lift at the far side. Their footsteps echoed as wet slaps through the large open space.

With the power still on in The Alpha Tower, Rhys saw the pools of blood as he ran through them.

"I know it's forcing us to look at this mess," Rhys said as they both ran through a particularly large pool, "but at least the power's still working in here."

Oscar nodded. "I'm guessing it runs from its own backup."

"Good job, really." Rhys pointed at the gold elevator doors. "We need one of these lifts powered so it can get us to the top floor."

CHAPTER 20

Once inside the lift, Rhys pressed the button for the fifteenth floor.

Nothing.

He pressed it again, harder and repeatedly.

He pressed it to the point where it stung his finger, but still nothing happened. He stared out through the open doors into the foyer; if a group ran at them now and pinned them in the elevator…

The buttons for floors twelve, thirteen, fourteen, and fifteen all looked the same. Embedded in the large gold plate like all of the elevator's controls, the top four glowed red instead of green.

When Rhys reached up to press the button again, Oscar grabbed his wrist and squeezed hard.

"Ow," Rhys said.

Sweat beaded Oscar's brow and he looked pale when he pointed at the card reader below the buttons. He struggled to get his words out. "I'm guessing they're red for a *reason*. Maybe you should use your security card and see if that helps."

A glance out into the foyer and Rhys fumbled for his security card. A need to hurry made his hands shake. His cheeks flushed as he felt Oscar's cold glare on him. *Of course, the card reader would give them access to some of the other floors. It made perfect sense. It wouldn't be there otherwise.* He'd looked like a complete idiot for the entire time he'd been around Oscar. No wonder the big man treated him with such contempt—that and the fact that Oscar was clearly a dick.

As happened with every card reader he'd come across, Rhys swiped Vicky's card through it and the small red light turned green. Not only did the light on the reader turn green, but the buttons for the higher floors changed to the same colour.

Oscar pressed the button to the fifteenth floor and the lift doors closed.

Just before the doors had shut out Rhys' view of the foyer, another diseased scream tore through the open space.

The hairs lifted on the back of Rhys' neck when he saw a solitary diseased appear. Its jaw hung so loose it swung as the creature jerked its head around. Blood streaked its pale cheeks and it had a deep gouge that ran down the side of its face. When it turned to the lift, its mouth stretched wide and it screamed again.

The thud when it collided with the other side of the closed doors made both Rhys and Oscar jump back. Seconds later, the lift rose. Rhys shook his head. "Great, we've got to come back down to that."

Oscar cleared his throat, but didn't reply. The act of riding in a lift together seemed to quash any idea of conversation. Rhys nearly conformed to that social convention until he looked down at Oscar's thigh. "What the fuck?"

The patch of blood had been large before, but now the entire top half of his trousers had turned red.

After he'd looked down at his leg, Oscar lifted his head again. Sunken eyes stared back at Rhys and he shrugged. "The fight in the foyer must have torn it open farther."

"Take your trousers off," Rhys said.

"Huh?" Oscar skin turned paler with every second that passed.

"Take your trousers off *now*."

Although Oscar looked like he wanted to argue, he undid his belt buckle and dropped his trousers.

Rhys balked and turned away from the fleshy, deep red sight. "Fucking hell, mate; I've seen some bad wounds today, but… *Fuck.*"

Oscar stared at Rhys but didn't reply.

After he'd placed his baseball bat and bag on the floor, Rhys retrieved Oscar's trousers. A quick check of the controls and he saw they'd passed the fourth floor.

Rhys then turned the trousers inside out and folded them over so one leg lay on top of the other. He pulled them taut and kneeled down. "Push the wound close together."

When Oscar forced both sides of the deep gash together, dark blood oozed from the wound. The large man shook and breathed heavily as he held it in place.

A look up at Oscar's sweating face and Rhys nodded. "You ready?"

Oscar nodded back.

Rhys found the cleanest patch on Oscar's bloody trousers and pressed that against the wound. He then pulled both sides of the trousers around the back of Oscar's thigh and tied a tight knot.

A glance behind and Rhys saw they'd passed floor number seven.

When he looked back up at Oscar, the big man breathed heavily and his face glistened. "It'll have to do," Rhys said. "I think it'll hold for the time being."

With a stoic nod, Oscar fell against the lift's wall.

As the lift continued to rise, Rhys retrieved his bag and bat. He slipped the rucksack on and squirmed beneath the discomfort of it. It sat lopsided on his back, so he tugged on the right strap to adjust the weight of it correctly.

Still out of breath from the exertion of the day, Rhys panted and looked at the lift's control panel. They'd reached the tenth floor. He removed the map from his top pocket and the wrinkled paper rustled when he unfolded it. The drawing said what it needed to. It left out one important detail, however. It didn't reveal which room had the controls in it. Oscar would have to believe whatever Rhys told him.

Oscar could clearly see the map over his shoulder, so Rhys lifted it to give him a better look. "When these doors open, we'll be at the end of a long corridor." The map shook in his hands and his palms sweated more than before. "The two rooms are at the opposite end," he cleared his throat and his face burned at the thought of the lie. He couldn't repeat it again.

Oscar said nothing.

When they passed the twelfth floor, the entire wall in front of them turned white. Rhys squinted against the bright light. It had black letters in the top left-hand corner that read 'FL15'. "That's where we're heading," Rhys said as he stared at the wall and waited for the screens to show him something more.

An image appeared in front of them and Rhys' blood ran cold. His tired limbs ached worse than before.

"It looks like we have a welcoming party," Oscar said. He

continued to lean against the wall and his eyes rolled in his head.

They originally looked small on the screen because they'd camped out by some closed doors a distance away, but the rising elevator seemed to pique their curiosity and both of the diseased got to their feet. As one, they charged forward. They bashed into one another and the walls in their attempt to be the first to the lift when the doors opened.

"Those things will be on top of us the second we reach the fifteenth floor."

Oscar sighed and lifted his axe. He looked like he could barely keep it aloft.

"I've got these two," Rhys said. "You just wait here, yeah?"

Oscar lowered his weapon and didn't reply.

Rhys turned to the door and readied his bat. His heart hammered an irregular beat as he looked around his confined space. His dry throat pinched when he swallowed. How the fuck was he going to get a good swing at them?

CHAPTER 21

With his bat raised, Rhys' arms trembled as he watched the elevator door. Another look to either side and he shook his head. He could barely move in the tight space.

When they stopped at the fifteenth floor, Rhys' heartbeat ran away from him and his breaths quickened. The rancid tang of the diseased filled the air before the doors opened. Rhys gulped when he heard the *ping* that announced the chaos about to enter their world.

The crack down the centre of the doors widened, and the diseased groaned louder as their excitement mounted.

With the gap at no more than a couple of inches wide, their two bloated faces pressed into it. Their eyes bulged and they snapped their teeth. One of them poked his tongue out as if the extra inch would get him to his prey sooner.

Rhys sneered; the vile protrusion reminded him of black pudding.

When the door opened wide enough, Rhys jabbed his bat twice through the gap. Each jab connected with the face of one of the diseased and they both stumbled back.

Before they could charge forward again, Rhys jumped out into the corridor.

With more room around him now, he swung for the first diseased. He caught it clean and the thing flopped.

Before Rhys had time to react, the second diseased hit him hard. They both fell to the floor, Rhys on his back and the thing on top of him. Rhys held each end of his bat like a bar and wedged it beneath the creature's chin. It pulled its skin tight, and forced its face away.

When Rhys glanced behind, he saw Oscar remained in the lift watching. The man looked better than he had moments before, yet he remained rooted to the spot and stared with a cold detachment.

When the diseased shifted on top of Rhys, Rhys adjusted the position of his bat so it remained locked beneath the thing's chin.

The diseased leaned over and snarled with a phlegmy rattle as it bit at the air between them.

The weight of the thing made Rhys' arms shake worse than before. No matter how hard he wedged the bat into its neck, it did nothing to subdue the desire with which it tried to attack him. The fucker didn't seem to care whether it could breathe or not.

Rhys stared into the thing's dark eyes. A film of blood still coated them, but they didn't actively bleed like the others. The red trails down its face had dried. It must have been one of the early ones to turn.

Rhys' arms shook worse than ever as he lost the strength to hold the thing at bay. When he took a deep breath, he inhaled its reek and said, "Oscar, help me *please*."

The thing on top of Rhys pushed down more, and Rhys thought about Oscar as he stood back and watched from the lift. He shouldn't have trusted him. He knew the guy was a psychopath.

The sharp snap of the diseased's jaws became more frenzied. It clearly sensed it had the advantage. It twisted and shook with renewed vigour. It screamed so loud it hurt Rhys' ears.

Rhys' arms gave way a little more. Just centimetres separated him and the rotten bite of the diseased. Rhys turned his face to the side and breathed through his mouth to combat the smell. The heavy, phlegmy rattle of his opponent wheezed in his ear. Its hot and rancid breath turned clammy on the side of Rhys' face.

A loud *thunk* that sounded like a dull bell had been struck, and the pressure lifted from Rhys' arms. The thing fell to the side and Rhys looked up to see Oscar above him. The diseased that had been on top of him cowered; it had taken a heavy blow to the head from the blunt side of Oscar's axe.

"Yahhhh!" Oscar yelled and drove the axe so hard into the creature's face, half of the blade disappeared into its nose. Oscar pushed against its head with his boot and ripped his weapon free with a wet squelch.

As Oscar examined his bloody axe, Rhys looked at the dead body next to him. It had a lab coat on. Despite the shake that ran through his exhausted arms, Rhys pushed himself up and rifled through the dead scientist's pockets.

Within seconds he'd found the guy's security card. The photo on it matched the man. Rhys looked at the corpse and said, "Thanks, Wilfred, just what we needed."

When Rhys pushed off against the floor, his arms nearly gave way. His legs buckled as he walked.

Rhys turned to Oscar—the large man covered in a fevered sweat—and said, "Thanks. Thanks for saving me."

Coldness sat in Oscar's gaze as he dipped a stoic nod. "It's okay."

The long corridor had been separated into sections with sets of doors. It seemed like each segment served as another area for quarantining the fallout from whatever wicked experiments went on in the labs at the end.

Large windows ran down either wall. Although the doors were at the end, they showed a lab on each side. "So this is it," Rhys said as he looked from one room to the other. "This is the place where it all started. Rather underwhelming when you've seen the severe consequences, wouldn't you say?"

Oscar didn't answer. Instead, he held his hand out. "You found a security card. Can I have one?"

Rhys gave him Vicky's card.

For a second, Oscar stared at it. "This is lower security than the scientist's one."

"Is it?"

"You *know* full well it is. Take the better card, fine, but *don't* mug me off."

Oscar may well have just saved Rhys' life, but the fucker took his fucking time about it. "Come on," Rhys said, "let's do this, yeah?" He walked up to the first security door and swiped his new card through it. The light turned from red to green and the door slid open.

Although he didn't move at first, when Rhys stepped into the next section of the corridor, Oscar followed him.

CHAPTER 22

The long corridor had been broken up by four sets of sliding doors. It created five sections that they needed to pass through. "This much precaution to prevent the disease getting out, and it *still* spread?" Rhys said. He shook his head as he swiped Wilfred's card through the reader at the second set of doors. They opened with a *whoosh*.

"You could have given *me* that card, you know," Oscar said.

Rhys moved onto the third doors and didn't reply. When he got to the card reader, he swiped the card and turned to look at Oscar. The tall man grimaced as he walked with a limp.

Rhys waited and looked through the doors. The corridor beyond, a brilliant white, had been splattered with blood. The dark red stood in stark contrast to the sterile walls and floor. Despite the warmth from the hot day, Rhys shivered. The place reminded him of a hospital. No matter how warm the actual buildings were, he *always* felt cold in hospitals.

"I've saved your arse on more than one occasion," Oscar

said when he caught up with Rhys. "So who made you the boss of me?"

"I'm not saying I'm the boss of you. I'm just not giving you this card." Although Oscar still stood as an imposing form, Rhys had seen the wound on his leg. If it kicked off between them, a quick blow to his thigh and Oscar would go down in a flash.

As they walked to the fourth set of doors, Rhys listened to Oscar's heavy breaths and staggered steps behind him. Rather than look at him, Rhys looked at the labs on either side of them. The one on the right looked like it hadn't been used in some time; empty beakers, test tubes, scales, and other scientific equipment sat on the sides. The one on his left, however… "Have you seen this, Oscar? It looks like the place has been turned over."

"Everywhere looks like it's been turned over."

"Yeah, but we're at ground zero now, aren't we? Somewhere on this top floor, the virus was created and unleashed." Rhys looked at the table toppled over in the middle of the room. Two chairs lay on their side as if thrown away from it. One of the worktops had been swiped clean like someone had run an arm across it. Then Rhys looked down and froze.

Oscar walked up next to him. "What's up?"

Rhys pointed to thick lump of flesh on the floor. "It looks like it's been cut out of someone on purpose."

"It has been cut out of someone on purpose."

Rhys gasped and turned to the pale man. "How do you know?"

"It's a *steak*, Rhys, and that someone's a cow. Jesus, what's wrong with you? Are you fucking *new* or something?"

Rhys looked at it again. "They must have used that to start this hot mess. I bet the steak was infected and someone was tricked into eating it."

"So what if they were? What does it matter now?" Oscar said. "It's happened; some scientists played god and it back-fired on them. Fuck, it backfired on all of us."

A look at his watch and Rhys said, "We're down to nearly two hours left. You're right; we don't have time to worry about where it's come from."

At the final door, Rhys swiped his card—the card that belonged to him now, and would always belong to him regardless of what Oscar said—through the reader. He stepped through and Oscar limped after him. The tall man needed Rhys more than he needed him now.

"You may not be *saying* you're the boss of me, Rhys, but you're *showing* it by not giving me that card."

Rhys ignored Oscar and looked at the two rooms in front of them. For a crude and quick rendering, Vicky's representa-tion of the corridor was functionally accurate. A set of double doors led to each room—in one of those rooms sat the computer that could free the city.

Each set of doors had large handles that needed to be pulled to be opened. The small windows on the front of each didn't reveal much of the room beyond. It was a good job, really. If Oscar found out about Rhys' lie too early…

Rhys throat dried again, but before he could say anything, Oscar barged into him on his way past.

Rhys rubbed his shoulder where Oscar had collided with him and watched him head for the room on the right. The large man pulled the doors wide and marched straight in.

Rhys slowed down as he waited for the doors to close. The second they did, he slid his baseball bat through the two handles. He watched through the small windows as Oscar, oblivious to what he'd just done, spun on the spot to look at the room.

As he walked back to the door, he shook his head at Rhys.

"There's nothing in here." The doors muffled his voice. "It must be the room next—" When he pushed the doors, they moved only slightly before the aluminium bat snapped tight and rattled against the handles. Oscar looked down and his face fell loose when he saw the bat. His cheeks glowed red and his eyes widened. "What's going on, Rhys? What are you doing?"

Despite the physical barrier between them, a surge of adrenaline hit Rhys. He shook and stepped back a pace. His voice wavered. "There's something about you that I don't trust."

The larger man turned a deeper shade of red, bit down on his lip, and shoved the doors. The bat snapped tight again. Spittle sprayed the window when he pressed his face into it. "Let me the fuck out of here. I *mean* it, Rhys."

Rhys shook his head. "There's nothing in that room of any use. The only reason I told you there was is because I didn't trust giving you all of the information. It looks like that was a good idea from the way you just barged through. It's the room on the *left* where all the controls are."

The baseball bat rattled again as Oscar kicked the doors. He stopped to take a deep breath. The action had clearly hurt him. "This isn't funny, let me the fuck out!"

Rhys shook his head again.

The anger turned into desperation when Oscar threw his arms up in the air. "But I've saved your arse so many times. Were it not for me, you'd have been infected a *long* fucking time ago."

"You saved me because it gave you what you *needed*, not because you wanted to save me. Although, I've yet to work out what your angle is. Do you want to tell me now, Oscar? If that's what your name is."

"What the fuck's that supposed to mean?"

Rhys didn't reply.

"Look, I *don't* have an angle."

"Bullshit! You talked about a brother whose name and building number you couldn't remember." He pointed at Oscar. "Don't think I didn't notice when you gave me a different building number for him the second time around."

Oscar glared at Rhys.

"You didn't want to go and see him to give him a heads up on what's going to happen—that ain't right. You used Vicky's name, yet I've never mentioned it before. You watched the diseased attack me in the corridor—"

"I *intervened.*"

"At the last minute. And you fight like a fucking Marine. Something's going on with you and I have too many things riding on this to let you fuck it all up. Too many people I hold dear are relying on me to get this right."

Oscar's eyes narrowed and he lowered his voice. "Maybe you should think twice about who you hold dear."

"Like who?"

"Like Vicky. What are you doing leaving that lunatic with your child?"

"What the fuck do you know?"

Calmness settled over Oscar's features. It sent an icy chill through Rhys. "Let me out and I'll tell you a little story about our friend Vicky. And trust me, Rhys, if she had my child with her, I'd want this information too."

CHAPTER 23

R hys turned away from Oscar and went into the room on the left. He'd had enough of the man's bullshit.

The two rooms had a thick window between them, and although Rhys could still hear Oscar as he walked up to the main control computer, he chose not to look at him.

"You're making a mistake, Rhys."

When Rhys touched the screen, it came to life and prompted him to insert a security card.

"Vicky's bad news; trust me."

Rhys spun around and stared at the man. About the same width as the brick wall it nestled in, the window between them looked like it could withstand a lot more than even someone as big as Oscar could give it. "That's the thing, *mate*. I *don't* trust you. That's our problem, isn't it?"

Rhys looked at the graphic on the screen that explained the card was being read before he looked across at Oscar again. The man paced like a tormented dog. Rage twisted his features as if his fury intended to writhe free of his body.

A button appeared on the screen that asked Rhys to press it if he wanted to deactivate the defence system. He pressed it. It then gave him three choices—the shutters, the order to incinerate, or both.

The window that separated Rhys and Oscar made a bass boom as Oscar banged against it. "You need to turn the order to incinerate off." With wide eyes, Oscar jabbed his finger in the direction of the computer. "I'm being serious, Rhys, turn it off."

"So *that's* your angle is it? Why the fuck would I turn the order to incinerate off?"

"Because you may not get off this island in time if you don't."

"I'll get out in time. Besides, if this island doesn't burn, then the virus could spread."

A press of the button and Rhys listened to thousands of clicks throughout the city as the shutters lifted. It sounded like huge dominos falling as the hard snaps rang out one after the other in quick succession. Anxiety tightened Rhys' chest. What the fuck would the city be like when he went back outside?

Once the sound had died down, Rhys did a quick scan of the room. A white lab coat had been tossed over the back of a chair. Rhys took it and walked back out into the corridor.

Without a look at Oscar, Rhys proceeded to thread the thick garment through the two handles above his baseball bat.

He tied the two ends of the coat together and slipped his bat free before he tested the door. It held. When he looked back up at Oscar, his stomach pulled tight and his jaw fell loose. "Fuck."

The taller man stood on the other side of the doors with a deep frown on his face and a gun in his grip. He had it pointed directly at Rhys. He spoke slowly when he said, "Open the fucking door, *now*."

CHAPTER 24

E very muscle in Rhys' body fell limp as he stared at the gun. He moved his jaw several times before he got the words out. "How did you get a *gun* into the city? Where the fuck did you hide it?"

Oscar threw his head back and laughed so hard it echoed in the small room. When he looked back at Rhys all of the humour had left his face. A sneer of derision lifted his top lip. The thick doors muffled his voice. "You don't think they can *actually* tell when people are using or carrying guns, do you?" A shake of his head and he snorted a humourless laugh. "You poor deluded man."

Panicked breaths ran through Rhys and he held back his reply.

"All I had to do was strap the thing to my back so no one could see it. The scanners are a lie they tell to stupid people. If enough idiots believe it, it becomes a fact. That's how the truth works, isn't it? But your government's built on lies, so maybe there's so many you just don't see them anymore. It's the great illusion that is democracy. They fill your head full of bullshit to keep you compliant. That way they never have to take responsibility for being the ones imposing the constraints on you. They blame their actions on terrorism, or the potential threat of war. They lead you a merry dance based on the things you fear most. If you see enough people killed by lunatics, you'll give up almost anything to remain safe. All the while, they create the illusion of choice and keep the framework big enough that you don't realise it's a complex web that you're trapped within."

"What are you, some kind of conspiracy nut?"

For a second, Oscar lowered his gun and looked genuinely sad. "I *almost* feel sorry for you, Rhys. I live in a system that's far from perfect, but at least I know who's fucking me up the arse. The system you live within is a convoluted mess of lies that tries to pass itself off as something democratic. But it's all bullshit. We're both slaves to those in power."

Rhys didn't reply.

"Anyway, back to the matter in hand," Oscar said as he jabbed himself in the temple with the index finger of his left hand. "Think about it, Rhys; how can someone scan for the production of weapons? It doesn't make sense."

"I dunno... I just thought—"

"But you didn't think, did you? You accepted what you were told like a good little sheep. You're a fucking moron."

Stillness settled over Rhys, and he looked straight at Oscar. "I'm not the one trapped in a room."

"No, but you are the one with a gun pointed at your face."

Rhys looked down to the left. With enough speed, he could dive out of the way. The small windows restricted Oscar's aim. He needed to react before Oscar shot. "You know what?" Rhys said as he shifted to the left, "I only locked you in that room because I had my doubts. I wasn't sure about you, and if you'd have kept your head, I would have unlocked the doors and we'd be on our way now. But you've shown your true colours."

"Are you forgetting that I'm the one holding the gun?"

"That may be true, but let's say you shoot me, what then?" Rhys walked over to the room on the left and pulled the door open. When he glanced to his right through the window that separated the two rooms, he saw Oscar had followed him with the aim of his gun. After he'd taken another lab coat from the floor, Rhys stepped back outside the room.

While he tied the handles of the room on the left as tight as the handles on Oscar's room, he said, "The only way out of either of these rooms is through one of these sets of doors. The windows are too small for you to climb through, so you *need* me. Shoot me and you ain't going anywhere, sunshine."

Although his shoulders sagged, Oscar kept his gun raised. "It looks like we have a stalemate then."

"How's that?" Rhys said.

"Well, if I shoot you, I'm fucked. If you leave, you're going to get a bullet in your back. It seems that the only way out of this is if you set me free and we go our separate ways."

"And you expect me to trust a man who's pointing a gun at me, do you? A lunatic who's going against his heritage and siding with a bunch of paranoid nutters in The East."

"Take a look around, Rhys; it was *your* government who made this weapon, not mine. All we're doing is making sure it never gets over to us by setting it free over here."

"So you killed the policemen outside the city?"

"Me? No. My colleagues? Yes. We needed to make sure the virus got out. They would have contained it before it had gotten off the bridge otherwise."

Rhys' temperature lifted and he shook as he shouted, "The virus reached my son's school."

A slight frown creased Oscar's features but he didn't reply.

After a deep breath, Rhys' rage settled a little. "And that's why you don't want the island to incinerate?"

"Naturally. We're turning your own weapon against you. You may as well say goodbye to your boy. You may as well say goodbye to everything."

Heat washed over Rhys and sweat stood out on the back of his neck.

"Anyway," Oscar said, "even if you do get out of the city —which I don't think you will—you're all fucked. The only way to survive what's going to happen over the next few days is to get out of the UK. The airports will be locked down before you get there and no one will be giving you a lift; you're not important enough. Face it, you're all fucked."

"You're full of shit, Oscar. You're desperate; that's where this is coming from. You'll say whatever you can to get out of that room. You've failed. This island will burn with you on it."

Although he pretended to be calm, Rhys noticed how the gun in Oscar's hand shook. "None of it matters anymore, Rhys. As you've seen with your own eyes, the virus is already out. And even if you manage to stop most of it from getting out of the city, your country's already fallen. You saw the helicopter, didn't you?"

The image of the naked man flooded back to Rhys... the way the diseased tore into him and how he turned in just a few seconds. The dark memory scrambled his thoughts. He shook his head to clear it. "What about that helicopter? What do you know?"

"You saw them picking up the diseased, yeah?"

Rhys stared at Oscar and didn't reply.

"They're taking them out into the UK and dropping them

at random points; they have been for the past few hours. A few of our choppers have headed over to France to start the virus in mainland Europe. It's going to spread whether you like it or not, and at some point you're going to see your little boy eaten alive. Or worse, he's going to see you eaten alive and will be left all alone. You never know; maybe cannibals will get to him before the diseased do." A wide smile stretched across Oscar's broad face when he said, "Maybe paedophiles."

A mixture of grief and fear wobbled Rhys' words. "I *trusted* you. I helped you get here."

"Shut up, Rhys, you delusional idiot. You wouldn't have made it here if it weren't for me. Regardless of how bad my leg is, you needed me as much as I did you."

A shake of his head and Rhys shifted to the left a little more. It narrowed Oscar's angle. "I'm not letting you out."

"Let me out of here or I *will* shoot you."

"No. I can't… not now." Another step to the left.

The gun shook worse than before in Oscar's grip.

When Rhys saw Oscar's finger tighten, he dove to the floor.

The loud bang of the gun seemed to shake the very walls of the building.

CHAPTER 25

R hys' ears rang as he lay on the floor. The sudden movement had triggered the pain at the base of his back from the bike crash. A dull throb resided around his coccyx; however, the searing agony of a hot bullet in his body seemed absent. He moved slowly, as if he'd been shot anyway. The shock had hit him hard. He then looked up at Oscar.

The large man worked his jaw in large circles. His ears clearly hurt. But more importantly, Rhys saw the grey splash on the unbroken window in front of him.

Rhys stood up, picked up his baseball bat, and stared into Oscar's cold glare. He laughed, "The glass, it's bulletproof. Ha, who's the fucking *idiot* now?" He pointed at the big man. "You're fucked in there, Oscar, and there's fuck all you can do about it. Although you should consider yourself lucky— burning's too good for you. I can think of many more ways to kill you that would be far more appropriate. Terrorists should have their balls removed without anaesthetic just for starters."

"*Terrorist*? You were the ones who created this cursed

virus. None of this would have happened if it weren't for *your* vile government."

Two slow steps forward and Rhys had closed the distance between them. The stained pane of bulletproof glass separated them.

In a blink, Oscar raised his gun again and cracked off another bullet at the window.

A flash exploded between them and Rhys recoiled from the loud bang.

The splash on the window, although darker, remained as just surface-level damage.

Before Rhys could say anything else, Oscar screamed and kicked the doors. Veins stood out on the man's thick neck as he savagely beat the barrier that kept him contained.

Each blow moved the doors ever so slightly before they returned to where they were. The lab coat's tight knot held them better than the baseball bat ever could. "There's no way you're getting out, Oscar. Face it, pal, you've lost."

Red-faced and wide-eyed, Oscar turned to the large window that separated the two rooms and shot it—a loud bang, a grey splash, but still no broken glass.

When Oscar lifted the office chair in the room, Rhys laughed at him.

Oscar threw it against the window and the thing bounced off it with a loud *crash*. When it came back at him, Oscar had to jump out of the way before it clattered on the floor.

Rhys watched the big man as he stood lame on the other side of the glass. "It looks like you've run out of options. Not so confident now, are you?"

So close to the window his breath turned it misty, Oscar watched Rhys for a moment. "You were quick to realise that the story about my brother was bullshit. I do have a brother, but he lives in Kent and doesn't have Down's. I imagine he'll be vomiting up his own blood before the week's out… if he even lasts that long." A grin stretched across his face. "You'll see the same happen to your boy soon, and when you do, think of me saying 'I told you so'."

Rhys wrung the handle of his bat but didn't reply.

"You fucked up by leaving him with Vicky, you know? Oh, and you were right about that too; you never told me her name. I've known Vicky for some time now. We go *way* back. She's not who you think she is, and you trusted her with your child… pretty fucking dumb, if you ask me."

Rhys' breath quickened. "What are you talking about?"

"Turn the order to incinerate off and let me out."

"No."

"I'm not telling you anything then. Let's just hope your boy's okay when you get to him, eh? Not that you're going to make it back through the city."

Rhys shook as he retrieved his walkie-talkie from his tight pocket. He took a deep breath to calm himself before he switched it on.

Static hissed out of the small speaker. No signal. Rhys pressed the button anyway. "Vicky, it's Rhys. Can you hear me?"

Nothing but static.

Oscar laughed. "Poor little foolish Rhys. The man who trusted too much."

"You're right, I did trust too much. I knew you were a bad egg from the start, but I ignored my gut feeling and that's on me. I should have cut you loose immediately, Oscar, you fucking prick."

"Brendan," Oscar said.

"What?"

"My name's Brendan. Tell Vicky that Brendan says hi when you speak to her. Watch her reaction."

Rhys frowned so hard it hurt.

"She was a good fuck, you know."

While he backed away, Rhys shook his head. He had to get out of there. Time spent with Oscar ate into the time he needed to escape. He looked at Flynn's Superman watch. Just over one hour and forty-five minutes before the city burned hotter than hell.

Oscar grinned and waved at Rhys as he backed away. "Bye bye, Rhys. You ain't making it out of this city before it burns. Not with the hell you've just released out there and not without someone to bail you out as much as I have."

"At least I have a chance, you sick fuck. You have none. Good fucking riddance, you horrible bastard."

The sound of Oscar, or Brendan, or whatever his fucking name was, chased Rhys as he ran down the corridor away from him. "I should have fucking shot you when we were in the lift."

Rhys stopped and turned around. "But you didn't, did you? And you know why?"

Oscar paced up and down as he stared at Rhys.

"Because *you* needed *me* to survive; that leg of yours is fucked and you couldn't last without me. Sure, you did bail me out, but with your leg as it is now, you're less than useless." Rhys headed for the first set of doors.

A string of shouted abuse preceded several more thuds as Oscar kicked the shit out of the doors. But Rhys didn't look back. When he got to the first quarantine door, he swiped his card through the reader and it opened.

After he'd stepped through, he waited for the door to close behind him, lifted his baseball bat, and looked at Oscar one last time. With gritted teeth, he yelled and smashed the small black box off the wall.

CHAPTER 26

O nce Rhys had passed through the last door at the end of the long corridor, he smashed the card reader from the wall as he'd done with the others. The brittle plastic shattered and tinkled on the ground. A black rectangular plate remained with wires that hung down from it like entrails.

The section closest to the lift stank from the metallic stench of blood combined with the diseased reek of rot. Rhys could almost taste it.

A glance back to the room at the end sent a chill through Rhys when he saw Oscar. The big man dipped his head and watched Rhys from beneath his brow while he rocked from side to side. *If he doesn't burn when the city goes up...* Rhys shook the thought away. It didn't serve him to think about it. Besides, how the fuck would Oscar get out of that room and off the island before it burned?

The lift doors closed most of the way, but bashed into the leg of the dead scientist lying half in the lift and half in the corridor. Then the doors opened again. Each time they opened, a pre-recorded *ting* punched through the silence. The repetitive sound rang as the final ingredient of the madness that surrounded Rhys. Like a broken child that did nothing but head-butt a wall, it needed someone to stop it.

When Rhys got close to the man, he looked at his name badge again rather than the deep wound in his face. As he lifted his feet, he said, "Sorry, Wilfred," and pulled him back.

The first tug didn't move the fat man. A deep breath and Rhys pulled harder. This time he moved, but only slightly.

After several more tugs, a layer of sweat stood out on Rhys' body and his shirt stuck to him. He put his foot in the way of the door so it didn't close and removed his walkie-talkie again. The hiss of static responded when he turned it on. He pressed the button. "Vicky? Vicky?" A loud wash of white noise answered him. "Fuck it."

THE CONFINED LIFT SMELLED AS BAD AS THE HALLWAY, IF NOT worse. No matter where he stood, Rhys couldn't avoid the sharp vinegar tang of decay. Although Rhys had fought the scientist in the hallway, Oscar had killed him in the lift and a large patch of blood had spread out over the floor.

Adrenaline shook Rhys' hand when he pressed the ground floor button. As the doors closed on the nightmare that had spawned this entire fiasco, Rhys took deep breaths. He'd not even begun to see the worst of it yet. Thousands more people released into the city could only end badly. The only way he could survive would be to take advantage of the early insanity. If he did, then maybe he'd have a chance… maybe.

Rhys' stomach tingled as the lift lowered with a monotonous whir. He checked his watch; one hour and forty minutes left for him to get out of Summit City.

When the button for the tenth floor lit up, Rhys rolled his shoulders and swayed from side the side. The diseased fuck who had tried to get into the lift when they went up would no doubt be waiting for him at the bottom.

At the ninth floor, Rhys chewed the inside of his mouth and waited. Oscar had said Vicky couldn't be trusted, but Rhys had trusted her.

Floor eight.

He'd trusted her with the most important thing in his world. What an idiot.

Floor seven.

Maybe Oscar said it to get under Rhys' skin. Rhys must've mentioned Vicky's name, which is where Oscar got it. The guy was imprisoned now and had a ticking clock on his existence. In well under two hours, he'd be burned to ash. He'd say anything to get out.

Floor six.

Wouldn't he? But what if he did know Vicky? What if there was something about her that she hadn't told Rhys?

Floor five.

Rhys rocked back and forth. She had the most important thing in his life with her. She could do anything to him.

Floor four.

A shake of his head and Rhys focused on the lift's descent.

Floor three.

Without the space to swing the bat, he held it horizontally with the thick end pointed at the doors; much like he had when they went to the top floor. With one hand in the middle and the other at the handle end, he had it ready to drive forward like a mini battering ram to smash the nose of the infected fuck on the other side.

Floor two.

She wouldn't do anything to Flynn. She could have fucked Rhys over at any point and chose not to.

Floor one.

The smug face of Oscar with his wide grin came into Rhys' mind's eye.

Ground floor.

Panic fluttered through Rhys' chest and he bounced on the spot. There'd best be no more than one diseased when the doors opened. He couldn't cope with more.

The 'G' button turned green and the lift eased to a gentle stop with a slight bounce. A light *ping* sounded out. Rhys drew a deep breath and stared at the crack in the door with unblinking eyes.

A gap opened up in it and the phlegmy death rattle of the diseased snaked into the lift with the reek of death. The stench caught in Rhys' throat and his eyes watered. He remained alert, ready to lunge.

The doors opened as if in slow motion. First, he saw one bloody eye, then two. A wide mouth hung beneath them. The thing snapped its jaws and butted the doors as if trying to ram through.

Adrenaline surged through Rhys, but he held back. If he attacked at the wrong time, it would be game over. The first blow had to count; he wouldn't get a second chance.

When the gap opened to about a foot wide, the thing lurched forward. It came to an abrupt halt as it crashed into the doors, its shoulders too wide for the small gap.

With a clenched jaw, Rhys pulled the bat back.

The door opened another inch and he drove the thick end of the bat forward. With his entire body behind it, he rammed it square into the centre of the monster's face.

A moist crunch and the creature yelled then stumbled backward.

Rhys jumped sideways through the gap into the foyer. His rucksack hit the doors, but he made it through.

Before the diseased could regain its senses, Rhys—his vision blurred from the stink of the thing—switched his grip on his bat. He wrapped both hands around the handle and drove a full-bodied roundhouse swing at it. Its head snapped to the side and its legs folded beneath it. It hit the ground so hard Rhys felt the thud through his feet.

Another swing—downwards this time—and Rhys cracked its skull.

A loud scream and Rhys kicked the dead thing in the gut.

It barely moved.

He screamed again and his voice echoed around the large foyer. "Vicky, you cunt," he yelled as he kicked it again, and again, and again.

"You'd best be looking after my boy." Each kick shifted it a few inches away from him.

Tears burned his eyes and ran down his cheeks and he continued to drive blow after blow into its midsection. "I swear you'll pay if anything happens to him."

Kick, after kick, after kick.

∼

RHYS' ANKLE ACHED AND HIS SHIN STUNG FROM THE number of kicks he'd driven into the corpse. Tears coursed down his cheeks and grief ran a heavy stutter through his breaths.

Rhys dropped his head and heaved a heavy sigh. "Please let him be okay. Please."

Rhys finally looked around to see there were no other diseased in the foyer. Good job, really—he hadn't given it any thought until then. Another fucking mistake like that and he'd be dead. *Get your head together, Rhys. Don't make Oscar right. All you can do is get to Vicky.*

He glanced at his watch. One hour and thirty-five minutes left.

When Rhys moved, his back ached again. Two long strides and he broke into a run. It would have to hurt for the time being; he couldn't slow down.

Rhys' footsteps echoed in the empty foyer and his back loosened up as he moved.

When he reached the main doors that exited The Alpha Tower, he dropped his shoulders and heaved a weary sigh. "Fuck it."

CHAPTER 27

When Rhys pressed his face to the small window on the door, his breath turned to condensation on the glass. It put a misty blur over everything. Shame it didn't dilute the insanity. He rubbed the glass clean with his sleeve and looked out again, careful not to press his face too close.

Chaos tore through the square exactly as it had earlier, but on a grander scale. There must have been ten times the number of people outside. The number of infected to uninfected weighed massively in favour of the uninfected, although that wouldn't last.

With no Vicky, and minus the psychopath upstairs, Rhys had to do this alone.

The sun had sunk lower in the sky. It would be a few more hours until it was dark, but the place would be a fiery mess by then anyway.

As Rhys searched the square in the hope he'd see a route through, he caught sight of Oscar's bike in his peripheral vision. It remained propped against the wall where Oscar had left it—it even had the Molotov cocktail in the drink holder still.

Maybe Rhys had a slight advantage over everyone else. After all, he knew what the diseased were capable of. Most of the people outside wandered the square, shell-shocked and panicked. Many hadn't even worked out that they should run. Instead, they searched around, wide-eyed and slack-jawed. The diseased picked them off with ease. One after another, they tackled those too slow to react and bit into faces and torsos. Even the ones who fought back fell quickly. With so many diseased around, the only way to survive was to run. Because Rhys knew that, he'd be a much harder target than most.

As Rhys watched events play out in the square, his lungs tightened, and his breaths grew shallow. Despite his theory that he'd be harder prey, he could still fall like any one of the poor bastards outside.

A deep breath and hard exhale did nothing to still his hammering heart. He removed Wilfred's card from his pocket and swiped it through the reader. The red light turned green and the door popped open. The hellish sound of a city dying rushed into the building.

As Rhys pushed the door wide, his entire body turned to gooseflesh.

CHAPTER 28

After he'd mounted Oscar's bike, Rhys paused for a second and stared across the square. The quickest route was in a straight line to one of the alleyways on the other side... as long as he didn't get taken out by one of the many diseased that stood in the way.

A tilt of his wrist and he looked down at his Superman watch. An hour and a half would have been a long time to get out of the city on a regular day, but with the insanity that surrounded him, and with Dave and Larissa to collect, it would pass in a heartbeat.

Rhys squeezed the bike's rubber grips and looked across the square. A spectator at present, he'd have to take the plunge. One bad decision and he'd be dragged into the carnage. The pedal ticked as he wound it back to get it into the correct position. With it high enough, he rested his foot on top of it. Before one of the diseased had the opportunity to see him, Rhys gulped a mouthful of warm, arid air, and pushed off.

Although he had the alleyway as his final goal, Rhys

focused on the next gap in front of him. He could only take one step at a time.

Two people screamed as they ran across his path and narrowly avoided a collision with his front tyre. Before Rhys could react, they were gone. His heart beat a frantic rhythm in the aftermath of his panic.

Rhys had to swerve to avoid three people who fell in front of him with a heavy thud. Two diseased had taken down an old man. His screams fell silent almost instantly.

When another diseased ran straight for Rhys, he lifted his foot from the pedal and kicked out hard. He connected with the monster's chest. It drove it back and diverted Rhys on a wobbly path, but he remained upright as the diseased fell.

With the shutters gone, the low sun bounced off the reflective windows and lit up Summit City. The blood on the ground shone like a layer of molten wax. At seemingly random points, it had pooled into large puddles. When he rode through one of the puddles, the bike's tyres threw blood up at him as a fine spray that he felt against his bare arms and hands.

The smell of the diseased hung heavier than before. It damn near choked Rhys as he rode. If it had levelled out, maybe he would become used to it, but with every passing minute, another person became infected and it smelled worse than before.

Rhys' weak legs burned as he pushed on, his jaw clenched hard. His eyes stung from his refusal to blink.

On the next sharp turn, Rhys hit a particularly slimy patch of blood and flesh. The back wheel of the bike kicked out, and Rhys' pulse spiked as he entered a wobbly battle to regain control.

With a jerk, he brought the bike into a straight path and focused on the alleyway out of the square. Any more sharp turns and he'd be on the ground with the diseased on top of him.

The wet slap of thrown punches joined the roars, screams, and cries around him. Rhys shut off to it as best as he could and kept his tunnel-vision focus on where he wanted to go. He'd travelled about twenty metres, and had about fifty left to the edge of the square.

Knocked down by a pack of crazed diseased, a woman crashed to the ground in front of Rhys. One of them latched onto the front of her neck, and as Rhys narrowly missed them, he heard the hollow pop of what must have been her windpipe. Before she was out of earshot, he heard a shrill gargle as she drowned in her own blood.

To Rhys' right, an older gentleman became prey to several children. All dressed in the same school uniform, they swarmed over the man and latched onto him. He screamed over their snarls.

Rhys passed the water fountain. The water had turned a deeper shade of red since he'd last seen it. It looked more like a blood fountain now.

Rhys stood up to ride faster. The bike stung the inside of his knees as it whacked against them. Wherever he looked, he saw someone taken down by a diseased. The ratio of infected to uninfected seemed to have changed. Rhys now belonged to the minority.

The roar of a woman caught Rhys' attention. When he looked over his shoulder, his legs almost stopped working. About his age, maybe slightly older, she ran straight at him. With her arms out in front of her, she moved quicker than he rode, despite her uncoordinated sprint. He had no chance of getting to the alley before she caught him.

CHAPTER 29

Rhys rode so fast the wind blew his hair back from his forehead. He fought against his weakened legs and pushed harder. Lightning bolts of pain tore through him and he yelled out, which helped him find more speed.

Yet when he looked behind, he saw the woman had gained on him. Every ounce of his energy went into his escape, but she moved faster than he did. He had no chance against her.

The effort turned nausea over in Rhys' stomach, and no matter how hard he breathed, he couldn't pull enough oxygen into his tight lungs.

When the quick slaps of the woman's feet against the ground stopped, Rhys turned around again to look. In mid-flight and with her hand stretched out, she'd jumped straight at him.

So close her fingers brushed his shirt, the woman failed to grab him, fell, and clattered into the bike's back wheel on her way to the ground.

The bike flick-flacked and Rhys fought to keep a hold of the handlebars as they snapped from side to side.

So caught up in his attempts to remain on his bike, Rhys didn't see the diseased in front of him until they'd collided. The shoulder barge into the creature ran a shock through him that sent a sharp pain across the base of his skull. The diseased he'd crashed into stumbled away from him.

The impact rescued Rhys and he straightened out. When he looked to see the diseased slowly get to its feet, he pedalled harder and focused on the alley.

As Rhys got closer to the edge of the square, the chaos thinned out a little. Although still surrounded by diseased office workers, taxi drivers, and even a builder in a high-visibility vest, he could see more space than before. A route to the alleyway opened up in front of him; ten more metres separated him and his escape.

With his focus on his exit, Rhys saw the pool of blood too late. Before he'd had the time to react, the back wheel spun and his legs slipped.

Rhys grabbed both handles again and managed to both hold on and remain upright. His pulse sped. *Focus Rhys*!

A metre or two from the alleyway and Rhys checked over his shoulder one final time. As if from nowhere, a horde of about twenty diseased—led by the man in the high-visibility jacket—had gathered and chased him. "Fuck it!"

A glance into the dark alleyway and a rock sank in his gut; something wasn't right. He should go down the next one, but he didn't have time. Rhys rode straight into the tight space.

The tick of the bike's chain and his own short breaths bounced off the hard surfaces that surrounded him. Maybe he could outrun those behind.

Then Rhys looked up and wedged his brakes on. The bike came to an abrupt halt with a loud screech.

About fifteen diseased had blocked his exit from the alley.

Each one looked freshly turned. Their eyes bled and their wounds gaped as each one focused on him. A look behind and the pursuing horde flooded in on his tail. They brought the roar of hunger with them.

Rhys looked at the crowd in front again. As if inspired by the furious mob behind, they set the air alight with their screams and ran straight at him.

CHAPTER 30

The alley may have been long, but the pinch of onrushing diseased from both ends narrowed it down fast. Despite the extra light that reflected off the thousands of exposed windows in the city, the onslaught turned the place dark. With his hand pressed against his chest, Rhys' heart boomed as he divided his attention between the diseased both in front and behind him.

The slathering fury reverberated off the tight walls and the stench closed in. He'd come all this way to get taken out in a fucking alley! He should have listened to his gut and gone to the next alleyway along.

With both of his feet on the ground and the bike balanced between his legs, Rhys leaned down and pulled the Molotov from the drink holder. His hand shook as he fished his lighter from his pocket and lit the rag. The flame ate into it and gave off black smoke.

A glance in front, one behind, one in front again, and Rhys threw the bottle behind him. They seemed closer. The glass smashed seconds before a loud *whoosh* of petrol roared through the tight space. A ball of heat then rushed at Rhys and lifted the hair on his head.

A layer of sweat stood out on Rhys' brow as he watched the flames force back the diseased behind him. Several of them screamed and raised their arms in front of their faces. The blood on their skin, and even their skin itself, hissed as the flames ate into them. The stench of rot mixed with that of charred flesh and the clothes of the diseased as they caught alight.

The diseased behind engaged in a fiery dance. Rhys shook his head to pull his attention away from the burning figures and turned to face the pack in front of him. As the mob closed in, he pulled his bag from his shoulders and rested it on the crossbar of the bike. A violent shake made it hard for him to even pinch the zip, let alone undo the bag. The diseased in front drew closer.

He finally got his bag open, and in one fluid movement, he removed one of the rockets, lit the fuse, and held it away at arm's length. He pointed it straight at the diseased in front of him.

The sparks from the back of the firework stung his hand like ant bites and the smell of gunpowder overpowered the stench of rot and seared flesh. He turned his head away and closed his eyes. The sound of the enraged diseased closed in on him.

The firework bucked and a loud *whoosh* shot away from him. Rhys opened his eyes to see a line of fiery colour run straight at the creatures. It stopped dead when it hit the first diseased directly in the chest. It caught in her clothes and kicked out a kaleidoscope of sparks. The other diseased backed away from it.

As Rhys removed another two rockets, the loud bang of the first one made him drop one of the fireworks. His ears rang and his head spun when he leaned down to retrieve it. The diseased in front of him backed away as one.

He held both of the rockets in one hand and lit them. Two kicks in quick succession, and they hurtled down the alley. One of them bounced off the close walls, but they both scored direct hits. Not that a direct hit was hard with the amount of diseased in front of him.

One of the diseased had taken a firework to the face, while the other took one to the groin. As the rockets fizzed and hissed on the floor, the mob backed off quicker than before.

Two more loud bangs sounded out.

The ring in Rhys' ears made it hard to hear anything else, but he already had four more rockets lit and pointed at the monsters. Two went off at the same time, the other two shortly after. All of them whistled as they shot down the alley.

The pack had already backed off to the point where they'd virtually cleared his way. The four rockets pushed them clear of the alley.

The flames from the Molotov had died down enough for the diseased behind to find their courage again. Rhys removed one more rocket from the bag before he threw his backpack—with the remaining fireworks still inside it—into the flames behind.

Bangs, fizzes, and pops issued from the bag, and Rhys lit the last rocket. The diseased behind backed away, some of them tripping over their own clumsiness in the haste of their retreat.

After he'd laid his baseball bat along the handlebars of his bike so it pointed straight at the diseased, Rhys then laid the rocket on top of the bat.

As he rode down the alley, the angry hiss of the rocket

culminated in a sharp buck that sent the firework off in front of him. His hand throbbed from the shower of sparks.

Rhys pedalled harder than before and dipped his head as he put everything he had into his escape.

He shoulder barged a couple of diseased on the way out. A weak hand tried to grab him, but he broke free of the confined space with no more than a slight wobble of his bike before he regained his balance.

The wide road on the other side of the alley didn't have the poles in the middle anymore, and although infected and uninfected fought in the streets, Rhys had more space to ride through than he'd had in the square.

Hopefully Larissa and Dave had made it through. Rhys couldn't wait in the city for too long. Trying to avoid the diseased was one thing, but he couldn't outrun instantaneous fire…

CHAPTER 31

When Rhys arrived at Central Station, he couldn't see another soul... infected or uninfected. The closest tower block was a few hundred metres away and the insanity hadn't spread this far... yet. But the possibility was that neither Dave nor Larissa had made it either and with the clock ticking towards incineration, he couldn't wait long.

Regardless of its apparent emptiness, Rhys rode over to the entranceway to the station and peered in. The escalators that led down into the seemingly abandoned tube station sat motionless, like they had earlier. If Dave or Larissa wanted to hide, they could have gone down there.

Before Rhys could venture any farther, he heard his name hissed from a dark corner.

"Rhys."

Dave stepped from the nearby shadows. Two tear lines streaked his filthy cheeks and he stared at Rhys through bloodshot eyes. The fire had clearly fucked him up.

"Are you okay, mate?" Rhys said.

Instead of offering a reply, his friend barked a deep cough

into his hand and nodded. As he continued to walk toward Rhys, he searched around with wide eyes and kept his voice low. "Why's it *so* quiet here?"

It did seem odd. "Dunno. I'm guessing we're too far away from any of the tower blocks for the carnage to have made it here yet. I think that's going to change pretty fucking soon," —another look at his watch—"although the city might be ablaze before that happens. Besides, the station areas are never busy unless it's rush hour. Who uses the trains at any other time?"

Dave looked far from convinced and continued his assessment of their surrounding area. "I think we'll be mobbed pretty soon if we don't get a move on."

For a second, Rhys stared at the space behind Dave before he looked back at his friend. "Have you seen Larissa?"

While he continued his perpetual search of everything around them, Dave shook his head. "No." The whites of his wide eyes flicked from side to side as if unable to settle on any one thing. "I don't like it here, Rhys."

"The entire city's fucked," Rhys said, "I'm not expecting you to like it anywhere, to be honest."

Dave's wild eyes finally settled on Rhys. "Where do you think she is?"

"Fucked if I know. She's probably turned into one of them. What are the chances of both of you making it here unscathed? But how can I go back to Flynn without his mum? I promised him I'd bring her back," Rhys looked at his watch again and shook his head, "but we can't wait for her. If we do we'll die, and I wouldn't mind betting that burning to death feels a whole lot fucking worse than being infected."

When Dave didn't reply, still clearly shell-shocked as he continued his wide-eyed assessment of their environment,

Rhys removed the walkie-talkie from his pocket. A twist of the power button and loud static hissed from the small speaker. Rhys jumped and shook in his panic to lower the volume. "Fuck!"

When he saw Dave stare at the loud device, he shrugged. "All I want to do is get a hold of Vicky."

"Vicky?"

A wave of his hand to dismiss the conversation, and Rhys said, "I'll explain later, but basically, Flynn's with her."

"You've left Flynn with a *stranger*?"

A look back to where he'd come from and the shrill call of the diseased ran a cold shiver down Rhys' back. "Now's not the time, Dave."

Before the conversation could go any further, a solitary figure rounded the corner. It ran at a full, yet clumsy sprint.

Rhys got off his bike and leaned it against a wall. With his bat raised, he turned to Dave and said, "You need to learn how to kill these things."

"But they're *people*!"

"They ain't people... very fucking far from it, in fact. They're monsters. If you think of them as human, you'll be one of them in a heartbeat." Rhys stepped forward when the infected woman got closer. She ran with her head dipped as if she were about to fall forward. Her greasy black hair swayed from side to side with the motion of her staggered gait.

Rhys took a deep breath and unleashed a full-bodied swing of his bat. The metal *ting* of it connected with the diseased's face. The sound rang out across the quiet city and drove the creature backward. A spray of blood shot away from her already bloody mouth in a long sticky line.

Rhys turned to Dave. "Now I'm sure this fucker's already dead, but once they're down, make *sure* you turn their lights out." While he bit down on his bottom lip, Rhys held the bat above his head and drove it into the skull of the downed creature. The bone broke with a *crack*.

When Rhys turned back to Dave, he saw his friend watch on aghast and said, "They ain't people any more. You need to get that into your head."

Before Dave could reply, Rhys looked at an abandoned car to his right. The front had a dent in it from where it had obviously collided with a pole. The driver's door hung open. Rhys walked over to it, leaned inside, and pulled the lever that unlatched the boot. A pop sounded out before Rhys walked around to the back of the car and opened it up.

After he'd pulled the carpeted board away and tossed it aside, Rhys looked down at the spare tyre. He then pulled the silver tyre iron out and handed it to Dave. "Here, use this."

Another heavy bout of coughs and Dave took the weapon. He bounced it up and down as if to test the weight of it before he stepped forward and hugged Rhys. He gripped him so tightly that Rhys struggled to breathe. "Thank you, man. Thank you for coming back for me. You didn't have to. I really appreciate it."

With his arms pinned to his side, Rhys nodded and moved his face away from the strong smell of smoke on Dave's clothes. "It's cool, honestly, but you need to give me my arms back, dude. I'm no good without them."

Dave let go and stepped back.

"Just promise me one thing," Rhys said.

"Anything."

"Don't freeze, yeah? I need to know you can kill these things if you need to. I need to know you have my back. Otherwise, you're putting both of us at risk. Do you understand? They ain't people anymore."

Dave nodded.

Rhys left his bike propped against the entrance to the station, and said, "Come on, mate, we can't wait for Larissa. We don't have any time left. I just hope she's made it to the drawbridge."

CHAPTER 32

Air moved in and out of Rhys' lungs much more easily than it had over the past few days. The relentless exercise seemed to have made a difference. Although compared to Dave, he had the fitness of an Olympic athlete, so maybe that was the difference. When Rhys had been with Oscar, it felt like trying to keep up with a racehorse, even with the big man's injury. Because Dave had spent the past few hours in a burning building, he coughed so hard that every few seconds he heaved. To be fair to him, he still ran while he coughed. Rhys would have stopped for sure.

Rhys talked as they ran. Dave listened and coughed some more. He'd only given Dave the briefest of versions but after a few succinct minutes, Dave had been roughly caught up on Vicky, Oscar, and the new information he'd been given about Vicky.

"So you still haven't got a hold of her?" Dave said as his feet slapped against the hard ground. A rattle accompanied his breaths as he pushed himself on.

Rhys shook his head and swallowed an arid mouthful of hot air. All he wanted was to stop and rest, but they had to keep going. Besides, if Dave didn't need to stop, then Rhys certainly didn't need to either. He glanced at the Superman watch; in under an hour and a half the entire city would burn hotter than hell.

With the drawbridge close, the pair pushed on. They'd made good time and they'd be on the river before the place went up. Hopefully Larissa would be there too.

"I've always admired you," Dave said before he broke into another coughing fit.

After he looked at his friend, Rhys looked ahead again. "Save your breath, man, you may need it if we run into a crowd of them."

"I just wanted to say it; you always get shit done." Sweat glistened on Dave's dark skin. It tore trails down his face where he'd been previously marked by the smoke and soot. He fought to catch his breath before he said, "If I had to bet on anyone coming to save me, it would be you. You put up with all my bullshit, but you still treated me like a friend. A lot of people would have cut me loose a long time ago."

A shrug and Rhys focused on his breath again. On a loop, he inhaled for four and exhaled for two. His lethargic steps played the beat by which he ran to.

"I'm so grateful you got me out," Dave said. "Thank you. You've always been the strong one. Level headed. We'd go out on the piss but you always kept your wits, no matter how drunk you got. And that's the thing. You never got wasted like the rest of us. You've got more class, man." Dave's voice wound tighter with each word until the inevitable coughing fit cannoned from him.

"*Save* your breath," Rhys said again.

Dave shook his head as he coughed. "You never got in fights. Never got so pissed you couldn't stand up. I was always a mess and you always held it together. And you know what? Even when you weren't out drinking with us, just seeing you in the morning kept me on a level. You always made me want to be a better person than I was."

Because Dave sounded on the verge on a panic attack, his breath so out of control he wheezed like a broken dog toy, Rhys tried to cut the conversation off. "Thank you."

But Dave drew another breath to speak and coughed harder than before.

Before Dave could say anything else, Rhys stopped and grabbed Dave's arm. Rhys pushed a finger to his lips and pointed up ahead. Dave looked up the road and got it straight away. When Rhys pulled him over to the side into the shadows, Dave moved without resistance.

As they waited, Dave still gasped for breath and Rhys watched him. He looked like he could cough again.

Out of breath too, Rhys kept his finger pressed to his lips. He sniffed the air. The reek of rot hung around them.

When Dave did the same, he screwed his face up at the smell.

Rhys pointed to the end of the street.

Dave looked like he did his best to stifle his cough and tucked in behind Rhys.

If his cough gave them away... Rhys didn't need to think about it. One step at a time. Only deal with the issues directly in front of him.

With Dave behind, Rhys walked forward and fought to bring his breath back under control. He walked towards the edge of the building on tiptoes. His weak legs trembled from the effort.

The closer they got to the bend, the greater the reek. The familiar stink of rot and excrement choked Rhys, and it felt harder to breathe than it had a few seconds previously. It didn't help that his throat had dried to the point where he felt sick. A funky taste of morning breath and bile sat as a furry layer on his tongue.

With the bend no more than a few metres away, the static hiss of Rhys' walkie-talkie cut through the silence. *Fuck!* He'd left it on from when he tried to call Vicky! Rhys heart leapt and he fumbled to remove the device from his pocket. When he'd finally managed it, he turned the volume completely down. It had been quite low anyway, so maybe nothing heard them.

He looked at Dave to see him chew his bottom lip as he stared at the black device in Rhys' hand. The guy still held his coughs back.

The pair stood in silence, stared at one another, and listened. Rhys watched the corner. One of the diseased would surely tear around it at any moment. He'd been worried Dave might give them away, but he'd left the fucking walkie-talkie on.

But it *was* Vicky on the other side. He *had* to talk to her. Rhys led a retreat from the bend. He *had* to speak to Flynn too. A quick conversation and they could head to the draw-bridge. But he had to have that conversation.

When they'd pulled back far enough, Rhys turned the volume of the walkie-talkie up again. A press of the talk button cut through the quiet hiss of static. Rhys' voice croaked. "Vicky, it's Rhys, come in."

"Rhys?" Her voice crackled through the small speaker.

"Why would someone from The East know your name, Vicky? What have you done?"

"I… I don't know, Rhys. I don't know what you're talking about."

"Why do you sound so fucking nervous then?"

Dave's mouth hung open as he watched on.

Vicky didn't reply.

"Brendan told me to say hi."

The hiss of static answered Rhys.

"Vicky? What the fuck's going on? What *aren't* you telling me?"

"I'm sorry, Rhys. I'm truly sorry. If I'd have known it would have come to this, I wouldn't have done anything, I swear. I'm so, so sorry."

Adrenaline surged through Rhys. It accelerated his pulse and pulled his guts tight. Just before he could respond, he saw Dave raise a shaky hand and point up the road. One of the group they'd smelled appeared from around the corner. But Rhys needed answers. "*What* have you done, Vicky? *Where's* my boy?"

"We've gotta split, dude," Dave said.

"*Vicky?*"

Nothing.

"*Vicky?* Where's Flynn? What have you *done* to him?" The walkie-talkie shook in his tight grip and Rhys' blood boiled. It took all of his effort not to smash the black handset on the ground.

Dave clamped a hard grip onto Rhys' shoulder, shook him, and pointed up the road again. "If we don't go now, we're fucked. Seriously, Rhys, we need to get a fucking move on."

Rhys looked up and saw the twisted, solitary diseased. It swayed from side to side as it walked. Oblivious until that moment, it turned and stared at the pair.

Time froze.

When the creature opened its mouth, Rhys' skin turned to gooseflesh. He'd pushed his luck and now they had to pay the price.

Dave spoke in a low voice, although the need to be quiet had already passed. "We *need* to go, Rhys."

Several quick nods and Rhys said, "I think you're right, man."

The creature released the familiar primal call of the diseased. A braying, heaving cry that told any of them within earshot *I've found prey*.

The pack answered with their usual thunderous roar.

Rhys and Dave ran.

CHAPTER 33

By the time Rhys had turned around, Dave already had a lead on him. The wheezy smoke-damaged Dave of only a few seconds ago seemed like nothing but a distant memory now. And because Dave had taken the lead, Rhys had to follow. He'd already opened up a gap big enough that he wouldn't hear Rhys if he called after him. The mob's feet behind beat a war cry against the pavement. If that didn't drown him out, their screams and roars would.

They couldn't run forever. They had to think of something. Or rather, Dave had to think of something; Rhys would have to go his own way if Dave made a bad choice.

When they rounded the next corner, a tower block came into view. Rhys' heart sank when Dave headed straight for it.

"What are you doing?" Rhys called after him, but before the words had left his mouth, he'd given up any hope of being heard. Instead, he ran and debated as Dave ran across the road to the other side.

Rhys' gut told him to run past the building. The tower block would be full of dead ends and nothing else. Unless Dave knew better than Rhys, that is. After all, the guy did run the building management for his last tower. Rhys often joked about him being no more than a janitor, but maybe Dave's knowledge would save them. Dave would trust Rhys' judgment in this situation. A shake of his head and Rhys crossed the road after him.

Like all of the other towers, Tower Eighteen's front doors had been flung wide open from the mass exodus.

Rhys entered the building about ten seconds after Dave. The large open foyer amplified both their hasty getaway and their heavy breaths. Dave barked a deep cough as he ran.

The front reception desk sat empty, the floor all around littered with blankets, cushions, cups, mugs, and other paraphernalia associated with a long fucking wait. After the initial fear had subsided, it must have been so dull to be locked up in one of the towers. Unless you watched hundreds of people burn to death, that is. Dave undoubtedly would have chosen dull over what he saw.

Dave looked like a man with purpose as he headed straight for the double doors on the other side of the room. A tilt to the side and he barged into one of them with a loud bang.

The door closed before Rhys got to it, so he did the same. The heavy door stung his shoulder from the collision and ran a shock to the base of his still sore back, but Rhys forgot the pain in an instant when he crashed into his stationary friend on the other side. "What the fuck, man? Why did you st—"

The drawn look of horror that hung from Dave's face robbed Rhys of his words.

Before he looked past Dave, he caught the rancid reek of rot. He heard the disgruntled murmur of what sounded like perpetual pain. He felt the combined focus of their collective attention. All of the hairs on his body lifted. At the end of the long corridor, aimless and restless, stood a herd of about fifteen diseased.

"Oh fuck," Rhys said.

As one, their dark mouths stretched wide, and they released the hideous braying call Rhys had come to think of as their war cry.

Being the closest to the door, Rhys spun on his heel and ran back into the reception area. He heard Dave follow but didn't turn around to check. His attention had locked onto the mob that had rushed in through the front door.

A door just next to the reception desk led down to the basement. Rhys ran straight for it.

As the mob descended on him, Rhys grabbed the handle and yanked it open. He checked to see Dave close and ran through.

A second or two later, Rhys heard Dave open the door behind him. When he turned and looked up the long flight of stairs, he saw his best friend slam the door shut and lock it. He then followed Rhys down.

The dark concrete basement reeked of damp. Humid and cold, it felt like they'd just locked themselves in a fucking dungeon. Rhys pushed on regardless.

Although Rhys had worked in an exact replica of this tower for years, he'd never seen the basement.

A loud bang and Rhys stopped to look up at the door again. One of the diseased had crashed into it and now pressed its face to the glass. It bit at it as if that would be enough to get through. The chink of its teeth against the glass called down into the darkness.

Several more thuds and more diseased fought for a space as they pressed up against the window.

Soon the thuds turned into hammered fists against the

door. They echoed and boomed like tribal drums. Like some kind of frenzied death ritual.

Rhys made it to the bottom of the stairs and looked at his watch before he looked back up at Dave. "It doesn't matter if that door holds or not. What matters is getting the fuck out of here. Where does this basement lead?"

With his attention on his feet, Dave descended the stairs.

"*Dave*," Rhys' raised voice echoed in the enclosed space, "*where* does this fucking basement lead?"

Dave still looked down when he said, "How the fuck should I know?"

"Because you ran a building before everything went to shit."

"That doesn't mean I've been in the basement. I never had any need to go down in one."

"And no one went down into one when your building was on fire?"

"No. We were too scared to get trapped down there."

"Well that's fucking *grea*t isn't it?"

When Dave made it down, Rhys looked back up at the small window in the door. The glass had turned red with infected blood. "Why the fuck did you lead us into a building?"

Dave fought to catch his breath and coughed several times before he said, "I… thought we could… hide from… them."

"What the fuck?"

"I don't know… I was scared. The tower seemed like the best place to run to. You were the one who led us down *here*."

A shake of his head and Rhys threw his arms in the air. "Well thanks, Dave. After all I've been through and I get fucked because I trusted your judgment." Rhys pointed up the stairs. "If those fuckers don't bust through, then the fire will get us."

Dave didn't reply. Instead, he stared at his friend, his eyes glazed with tears.

Rhys turned his back on him and watched the diseased at the top of the stairs.

After a minute or so, Rhys said, "Look, mate…" but when he turned around, Dave had vanished. "Dave?"

A moment later, Dave poked his head up from a dark corner. A wide grin spilt his face.

"What are you so fucking happy about?"

"Come and take a look at what I've found."

CHAPTER 34

"If I follow you, who's going to keep an eye on them up there?" Not that Rhys could see the diseased through the window anymore. Instead, he watched the blood currently smeared over it shift and change as faces, hands, and whatever fucking else rubbed against it. "We *need* to be ready when they get through."

While he continued to grin at him, Dave shook his head. "No we don't, Rhys. Just come and look, yeah?"

Another look up the stairs and Rhys shook his head while he walked over to Dave. The basement was so poorly lit that he only saw the stairs when he got close to them. Not as long as the ones they'd just descended, they ran a steep drop into an even darker space. Rhys shook his head. "What the fuck? Where do they go?"

"Follow me," Dave said and coughed several times before he ran down the stairs.

Rhys' legs ached as he followed his friend. The smell of damp increased the lower they went. The air grew teeth as the coolness nipped at him through his thin shirt.

When they reached the bottom, a huge space opened up.

About the same dimensions as an Olympic swimming pool, the concrete area had very little to offer. "What are you so fucking excited about?"

Dave looked across at the far wall.

When Rhys noticed it, he drew an involuntary gasp. The wall had a door in the centre of it. "Where does it go?"

"Fucked if I know." After he'd coughed into his hand several times, Dave said, "However, I did just open it. It's more than a cupboard. Anything's better than going back the way we came, isn't it?"

Rhys tilted his head so his ear pointed up the stairs. The bangs seemed to increase in ferocity, almost as if their disappearance fired up the diseased's rage even more. Then he heard the pop of the window as it broke. The rush of glass hit the concrete steps on the other side and the screams of the infected flew down into the basement. When he looked at his friend's wide eyes, Rhys dipped a sharp nod and said, "Let's go."

CHAPTER 35

After Dave opened the door, Rhys peered into the tunnel. He could only see a few metres in front of him before the darkness became impenetrable. He called into it, "Hello."

His echo responded.

When he looked at Dave, his friend stared back at him, dumbstruck.

"What do you think?" Rhys said.

The sound of splintering wood came down to them from the door up in the reception area. After he'd looked in the direction of the stairs, Dave said, "Do we have any other choice?"

It made sense. Of course it made sense; they had five minutes at the most before a flood of chaos came down the stairs at them. Nevertheless, that didn't make the prospect of a dark tunnel any more exciting.

Rhys poked his head inside the tunnel. Damp hung heavier in the air down there than in the basement. The temperature seemed to have dropped by a few more degrees. Rhys shivered.

Another crash, louder this time, and the sound of the diseased's feet descended the stairs. Within a few seconds, the ground shook.

"It's like a fucking *army* coming for us," Rhys said. His nerves jangled.

Without another word, the pair darted into the tunnel, slammed the door shut, and Dave lit up the space with the torch on his phone.

"Thank god you've still got your phone," Rhys said. "I dropped mine ages ago. I didn't fancy running down here blind... especially with those fuckers chasing us."

Rhys pointed his baseball bat at the door they'd just closed. "Put your light on that will ya."

Dave lit it up.

An overhead swing of his bat and Rhys knocked the door handle clean off in one hit.

"What are you doing?" Dave said.

A tight pinch on the square rod that connected the handles, and Rhys pulled it free. A metal *chink* sounded on the other side of the door as the handle fell to the floor. Another metal *chink* responded when Rhys dropped the rod on his side of the door. "It'll slow them down if nothing else."

"Ah," Dave said as he patted Rhys on the back, "clever. That's why you're the brains and I'm the looks."

An arched eyebrow and Rhys shook his head. "Whatever, Casanova. Come on, let's go."

THE MEN COULD JUST ABOUT RUN SIDE BY SIDE DOWN THE cramped tunnel. A huge metal pipe, about a metre in diameter, ran along the wall in the top right hand corner. It limited the height on one side of the tunnel, but not to the point where either man couldn't run beneath it.

Before they'd gone far, Dave suddenly stopped. "Look at this, Rhys."

Reluctance weighed heavy on Rhys' limbs, but he turned around and ran back to his friend. When he saw it, his breath left him. "Fuck."

Before he could say anything, Dave fell into another round of heavy coughs. The bark from his chest went off like a grenade in the tight tunnel. When he'd finally finished, he said, "It's a map, Rhys."

"I can see that."

"The buildings are interconnected."

"I can see that too." As he scanned the map, Rhys ran a finger across it. He felt the damp that clung to the walls. "We're not far from Building Thirteen. If we can get there, we can get to the drawbridge easily."

"We're going to get out of here, Rhys. We're going to do it, man."

A scream sounded outside the door like a firework rushing toward them. It culminated in a loud bang as the first diseased crashed against it.

Both Rhys and Dave jumped back and stared at it.

"Come on," Rhys said, "if we're going to get out of here, we need to go now."

The pair took off again. Dave's torch threw a hectic light around the place as his arms pumped. It brought the shadows to life and made it hard to see the way; not that it mattered in the mostly straight corridors.

∾

WHEN THEY REACHED ANOTHER DOOR, RHYS' HEART SANK. "I knew it was *too* fucking good to be true. I bet it's fucking locked." But when he turned the handle, the door opened.

Both men rushed through and Rhys did the same to this door as he'd done to the last. Again, he pulled the rod through to make it harder for the mob to follow them. Again, the handle on the other side fell to the ground with a *chink*.

As Rhys and Dave ran, their laboured breaths bordered on embarrassing. Rhys may have been slightly fitter, but the pair of them still sounded like old asthmatics. It didn't matter though; Flynn needed him and he'd push himself to collapse if he had to. If he could find Flynn again, that is. Rhys shook his head. It wouldn't do to think about it now. Once they'd crossed the river, he'd get to his boy. *If Vicky's done anything to him...* He shook the thought away again.

At the next door, Rhys paused and listened to the call of the diseased. Although distant, it still gained on them. "They're still chasing us. I'm pretty sure they've made it through the first door." He pulled the next door closed and smashed the handle off.

Before they set off again, Rhys heard the sound of rushing water. He reached up and placed his palm against the large metal pipe. It felt cold to touch. Condensation coated the outside of it. "No wonder the entire place reeks of damp."

"Huh?" Dave said.

The pipe vibrated from the heavy water flow that ran through it. A couple of jabs with the end of his baseball bat and the pipe boomed. "Hear that? That's the sound of a full pipe."

"Full of what?"

"Water, I'd guess."

After a slight pause, Dave said, "So what? Come on, man, we've got to go."

The diseased's screams grew louder and Rhys glanced at his watch. The hands glowed in the dark. In just over an hour, the entire place would be turned into one of the layers of Dante's inferno.

CHAPTER 36

As the pair ran, the wet slaps of their feet against the ground and the distant cry of their pursuers were the only sounds in the dark tunnel.

When they got to a door on their right, they stopped as one and Dave shone his torch on it. He moved his torchlight to the wall next to it and lit up another map. Dave read the writing across the top and his voice echoed in the hard space. "Building Fifteen." He coughed several times. "We're only one away. Thank god. This place gives me the *creeps*."

They passed through another door that barred the way and Rhys smashed the handle from it like he had on all the other doors. The loud *crash* of it went off like a gunshot. A pull on the rod between the two handles and he listened to the metal *ching* as the handle on the other side hit the floor. The diseased screamed almost as if they understood his actions and knew their way would be barred again; although, their distant cries rang fainter than before.

"Good job, mate," Dave said, "I think the doors are slowing them down."

The pair set off again.

Within a minute or so, a stitch tore up Rhys' side like he'd been stabbed. He raised a hand at Dave while he slowed down. "We have to ease up a little, man." He hooked a thumb over his shoulder. "They're far enough behind."

Dave slowed down, but a haunted look drifted across his face. "They'll never be far enough behind." He covered his mouth to stifle a cough.

The men moved at a fast walk. The pain in Rhys' side forced him to hold his ribs as they went.

"Thanks again for rescuing me," Dave said. "I know you think I'm a fuck up—"

"I don't think you're a fu—"

"It's okay, Rhys, you're right. I've been doing fuck all with my life. Drifting for years and living like I'm still a teenager."

When Rhys opened his mouth to respond, Dave cut him off again.

"But that's going to change from now. No more. I'm not going to be that loser who's always up for a night out and doesn't get out of bed on the weekends until after dark. What's fucking *wrong* with me? I'm an adult, so I need to start behaving like one. I'm going to ask Julie out."

"Now steady on, Dave."

"I'm serious. I want to settle down. Start a family. I want to try on some responsibility. Engage with my emotions rather than get wasted so I don't have to. I want to be a dad. Have kids who can be proud of me. It's time to grow the fuck up. You've handed me a second chance, and I'm going to grab it with both hands. I'm going to live every fucking second like it matters, rather than run away from it."

Rhys looked at his watch. "We've got to get off this island first."

"We will."

Anxiety stirred in Rhys' bowels. Dave clearly didn't get just how much more they needed to do to get free.

After he held the next door open for Dave, Rhys stepped through, closed it, and smashed the handle clean off. The loud whack boomed in the enclosed space and the diseased behind them screamed again, fainter still. "I know we're putting distance between us and them, but I don't understand how they're still on our tail," Rhys said. "What are they doing, tearing the fucking doors from their hinges or something? How have we not lost them yet?"

"We're moving quicker than them," Dave said. "That's all we can focus on. It won't be long before we don't hear their screams any more. Besides, we're nearly at Building Thirteen. After that we can leave the fuckers down here."

At that moment, the bright glow of Dave's torch dulled. The darkness that surrounded them grew as if it had been waiting for the opportunity.

When Rhys saw Dave stare at the screen on his phone, his shoulders tensed.

Dave looked back at Rhys. A frown darkened his brow as he said, "Oh shit. My batt—"

The light on the phone died.

The inky blackness that smothered them pushed against Rhys' eyes as if to claw even the memory of light from them. Another scream called out behind them. Rhys' own voice sounded louder in the darkness.

"It's almost as if they can smell the opportunity."

CHAPTER 37

The spark of the flint for Rhys' lighter punched through the darkness. One, two, three times before the flame took. A slight breeze—neither man knew where from—shook the tiny light and animated the shadows that surrounded them.

Blind spots flashed in Rhys' vision from the sudden change in light, and after a few seconds, he had to let the flame die. Hold it for too long and the plastic that held the strike wheel would melt, the spring-loaded flint would push against it, and the strike wheel, flint, and spring would disappear into the darkness forever. Better to have momentary flashes of light than none at all.

The men continued to walk at a fast pace. The darkness made Rhys move with greater stealth. Because of his lack of vision, he needed to keep his noise down so he could rely on his other senses. If only Dave would stop fucking coughing then maybe he'd hear something.

Every time Rhys stepped forward, uncertainty flipped his stomach in anticipation of a fall. At some point, he'd walk into something that would throw him to the ground. They didn't have any other choice but to keep on though; if they stopped, the diseased would catch them.

Rhys quickly gave up on his attempts to keep quiet. Their feet scraped as they shuffled along. It joined the sound of their heavy breaths, the rush of water in the huge pipe next to them, Dave's coughs, and the echoing screams of the diseased behind… It felt like they were trapped in a labyrinth with a Minotaur on their scent.

Every ten seconds or so, Rhys flicked his lighter. It punched through the darkness and the bright spark made him flinch each time. He half expected to see a wall of diseased in front of him in the brief moment of illumination.

A few seconds later and he lifted his thumb away from the lighter and plunged them back into darkness. Rhys finally spoke. "They're going to catch us at this rate."

Dave breathed in short, sharp bursts, but said nothing in response. Maybe he had a cough in his throat that he didn't want to release. Maybe he had nothing to add.

Rhys passed through another door and handed his lighter to Dave. "Here, keep this on for a second."

Dave lit up the tunnel and Rhys took a heavy swing at the door handle. It couldn't have been louder than any of the other handles, but the bang this time sounded like he'd fired a cannon in the tunnel and the darkness amplified the noise.

The pair moved off again and Rhys took his lighter back.

After another scream behind them, Dave said, "We can't be far. Once we get to Building Thirteen, we can get upstairs and get off this poxy island."

"And then the fun begins," Rhys said with a sigh. Just the thought of it made his heart hurt.

"What do you mean?"

"Vicky! Who the fuck is she? What has she done with Flynn? I swear, if she's harmed him…"

"We can't think about that right now, man."

"It's *all* I can think about."

Dave's hand landed on Rhys shoulder and squeezed it. He didn't say anything else.

Rhys fished his walkie-talkie from his pocket and flicked it on. For what good it would do. The sharp hiss of static bounced off the hard and close walls. Rhys depressed the button. "Vicky? Vicky?"

Nothing.

He put it back in his pocket.

When Rhys flicked his lighter on again, he saw another door barred their way. Like with all of the other doors, they stepped through it. Rhys gave the lighter to Dave again to light up the handle while he bashed it off.

A quick sweep of the area with the tiny flame and they saw another door. This time it was in the wall rather than in front of them. The pair walked over to it, and Dave handed Rhys his lighter back yet again. When Rhys flicked it on again, he smiled.

Dave looked at the door to Tower Thirteen and the sound of panic that had ridden his words abated as he said, "We're here, Rhys. We've done it."

Another distant roar called after them from way behind. After he'd looked back in that direction, Rhys sighed. "Thank god."

Rhys held the light up while Dave snapped the handle down and pulled the door open. Before Rhys could look in, the scream of the diseased rushed out.

In one fluid movement, Dave slammed the door and brought his tyre iron down on the handle with a sharp crack. The handle fell to the ground. Like Rhys had done, Dave removed the connecting rod and a chink sounded out as the other handle hit the ground on the other side.

When Dave finally turned around to face him, Rhys shrugged, "What the fuck are you doing?"

"Stopping them getting to us."

"But you're stopping *us* getting out."

"I ain't stopping us getting out. *They're* stopping us getting out. There are *hundreds* of them up there, Rhys."

"Fuck!" Rhys said and kicked out at the damp wall next to him. A sharp explosion of pain ran through his foot that turned nausea over in his stomach. "Fuck it! Fuck it! Fuck it!" The hands on his Superman watch glowed in the darkness. "We don't have much more time to get off this damn island. Fuuuuuuuuck!"

His call echoed away from them. The call of the pack behind responded. Their cries filled the hallway.

"We have to move forward," Rhys said. "If that means coming up through another building then so be it. The main thing is getting to the surface and getting away from both the diseased behind us and the ones in Tower Thirteen."

When Rhys stepped forward, he stopped instantly at the sound of more diseased up ahead. His blood turned to ice. "What the fuck was that noise?"

Dave's voice warbled when he replied. "There's more of them up ahead, we're *surrounded*."

CHAPTER 38

Even though Rhys couldn't see him, he heard Dave as he paced up and down. After several particularly heavy coughs, to which the diseased on all three sides of them responded with their cacophony of fury, he said, "What the fuck are we going to do? They've *boxed* us in, Rhys. We're fucked."

"The diseased behind us still have a distance to travel. There must be at least three to four doors between us and them. The door to Building Thirteen is stopping those fuckers in there. It's just the ones in fr—" The scream from in front of them finished Rhys' sentence for him.

Rhys flicked his lighter on and saw a door just up ahead. Like he had with all of the other doors, he bounded over to it and lopped the handle off with a swing of his bat. He swung from memory, but the satisfying *chink* of the metal handle sounded out as it hit the concrete ground.

Dave's voice turned shrill, "What the fuck are you *doing*, Rhys? We've got no way out now."

"That was *never* a way out," Rhys said.

The creak of splintering wood came from the door to

Building Thirteen. Seconds later, a loud thud boomed as the ones in front of them hit the barrier Rhys had just created. The ones behind hadn't caught up yet.

"What are we going to do?" Dave said.

The darkness made it harder for Rhys to keep hold of the panic that threatened to run away from him. The lack of visual distraction left him completely caught up in his head. Diseased screams came at him from every angle. He struggled to hold a straight thought.

Another creak of splintering wood and Rhys flicked his lighter on again. He held his hand out to Dave. "Give me the tyre iron."

Dave handed it over without complaint and took Rhys' bat in exchange.

When Rhys whacked the water pipe, the vibration shook all the way to his elbows and a deep boom sounded out.

"What the fuck are you doing?" Dave said. "Do you realise how much water's running through that thing?"

"Yes, that's *why* I'm doing it."

"Are you trying to drown us or something?"

"No, I'm trying to drown them." Another swing at the pipe and another loud boom. When Rhys sparked his lighter, he saw he'd made a large dent in it already. "They can't swim, but we can."

"But we can't breathe under water."

The two doors with the diseased at them held. The ones behind still hadn't caught up. Another heavy thud that sounded like a horse had kicked a stable door, and the door to Building Thirteen splintered again.

The faltering barrier creaked and groaned under the onslaught of the diseased as they tried to get at them. Rhys said, "How many did you see in there?"

"It looked like hundreds."

The door cracked again as it continued to give.

Rhys hit the pipe once more and a cold jet of water crashed into his chest. It came out at such a high pressure, it stung. So frigid, it burned.

A large lump of wood flew free from the door to Tower Thirteen and clattered against the floor. The vinegar reek of the diseased flooded into the tunnel along with their phlegmy rattle as their frenzy increased.

Rhys turned his back on the water and sparked his lighter. Bloated faces pushed through the large gap they'd already created. Bloody eyes glared and rank jaws snapped. Rhys watched them for a second.

Panic rode Dave's words. "What the fuck are you *waiting* for?"

He may have had a plan, but that didn't curtail the palpitations that ran through Rhys. With a tight chest that restricted his breaths, Rhys bounced on the spot and watched another panel come away from the door. "I need to time this right."

"Too fucking right you do. Leave it much longer and we're fucked. Hurry up, Rhys."

Another jet of water shot from the pipe and hit Rhys in the back of the head. "If I let the water out too soon, then we ain't getting out of here. They need to bust a hole in that door big enough for us to swim through before I set it free. I hope you're a good swimmer."

Dave didn't reply.

One more crack of splintering wood and the hole in the top of the door grew big enough for the first diseased to climb through. The flickering flame in Rhys' hand threw strange shadows off the thing as it bit at the air and slithered through the gap. The tightness of the space pinned its arms to its side until it fell, face first, onto the hard concrete with a wet crack.

At that moment, the spark wheel on Rhys' lighter pinged away from him and cast them into total darkness. "Fuck it!" Rhys threw the broken lighter to the floor and then turned on the huge metal pipe.

He screamed as he drove blow after blow against it. Each whack opened a bigger hole. More and more water rushed through the gap, soaked Rhys, and stung from the pressure it hit him at.

The final whack sent a heavy rush of water from the pipe that pushed Rhys first into the wall behind him, and then ripped his feet away from under him.

CHAPTER 39

A shock jarred Rhys' body when he hit the hard ground. It ran through his bones like a jab of electricity and turned the screws on the pain at the base of his back. The cold water from the pipe smothered him. It pinned him to the floor with an ice blast. Every time he opened his mouth to breathe, it filled with water.

It didn't matter how much Rhys twisted, the stream held him in place. His heart beat so hard it felt like it would explode.

The water stung his hands when he lifted them in front of his face, but it blocked the flow enough for him to turn to the side and steal half a breath. The breath had more water than air, but at least it had air.

Rhys coughed and spluttered as he rolled away. With the aquatic deluge, he had to fight for every breath.

The water had pooled on the floor already. The locked doors on either side clearly did enough to contain the flood as the levels rose.

The rush of water drowned out even the sound of the diseased. Rhys shivered as the coldness cut to his bones. He fought against his muscles' natural inclination to lock up. Pitch black and disorientated, he'd recovered his breath at least. He reached out to try to find his friend. He shouted so loud his throat hurt, "Dave? Are you okay, man?"

Now he'd gotten clear of the rush of water, he heard the diseased screams but nothing else.

When Rhys found the rough wall on the opposite side of the pipe—the wall with the door to Building Thirteen in it—he pressed his back into it and waited. The water had lifted to his calves already and it continued to rise.

Not only had the diseased's screams endured, but their acrid stench remained too. The hole in Building Thirteen's door had been smashed big enough for him to get out. With any luck, the one diseased that had slipped through had drowned already.

With the sound of the diseased by his side, Rhys couldn't wait around for more to get through. He stepped forward with his hand out in front of him. When he touched the cold pipe, he pulled the tyre iron back and swung at it.

Several more heavy blows and the pipe split. Rhys jumped to the side in time to avoid the jet of water. As pressured as the last, it shot across the tunnel. The gargled screams of the diseased told Rhys he'd scored a direct hit.

Rhys returned to the wall next to the door, pushed his back against it, and listened to the diseased from Building Thirteen lose their battle against the heavy flow.

For what good it did, Rhys shouted again, "Dave, if you can hear me, we need to wait for this section of the tunnel to fill up to the top. We need to make sure those fuckers have drowned before we try to swim through."

Rhys then stood still and waited as the water rose quicker than before.

WITHIN WHAT FELT LIKE LESS THAN A MINUTE, THE WATER had reached Rhys' thighs. The loud gush of it echoed in the small chamber. He shook to the point where the rattle of his own teeth played an erratic castanet beat through his skull.

When something grabbed Rhys, he jumped back and raised his fists. He'd have to fight blind. The water took away his ability to hear or smell his enemy too.

Then he heard Dave's voice. "Rhys; it's me, man."

The next time he felt hands touch him, Rhys reached out, grabbed them, and pulled his friend close. He held him in a tight hug. "Thank god you're okay. We need to wait for this place to flood to the point where it drowns those fuckers in Building Thirteen. Then we can go, okay?"

Dave didn't say anything.

"It'll mean waiting until the last moment before we make our move."

The water had already risen to his groin.

"Just follow my lead, Dave, okay?"

"Okay, man. You've got me this far."

Rhys' stomach tensed. He didn't need to be responsible for Dave's existence as well as his own.

WITHIN A FEW SHORT MINUTES, THE WATER HAD RISEN TO Rhys' chest. It wrapped him in a rigid straight jacket of cold that burned all the way to his heart. The diseased continued to beat at the door, but with less frequency, and less ferocity. The water had finally overpowered them. Occasionally Rhys heard another loud crack as they, or the water, obviously made the hole in the door bigger.

Rhys held himself in a tight hug, and the icy water forced rapid and shallow breaths from him as he listened to it rush through the gap into the basement of Building Thirteen.

When Rhys reached out to Dave again, he caught nothing. Another try and his hand found only cold water. "Dave? Where are you, Dave?"

Nothing.

"Dave?"

Still nothing.

Rhys' heart beat hard as the water rose. "Dave?" The loud rush continued unabated.

Surely, it hadn't pulled Dave under... but maybe the diseased fucker that fell through had.

THE WATER LEVEL HAD CLIMBED UP TO RHYS' CHIN. IT HAD turned his arms and legs numb. It had risen slower because it obviously had to fill Building Thirteen's basement as well as their tiny space. The sound of splintering wood had stopped. Rhys couldn't know any more; maybe the diseased had retreated, maybe they'd drowned. Either way, the water levels had risen to the point where he would have to take action soon.

As long as Rhys could breathe, he would wait. If Building Thirteen had the same layout as Building Eighteen—as it should—then the entire basement would be flooded soon.

A SMALL POCKET OF AIR REMAINED BETWEEN THE TOP OF THE water and the ceiling. Rhys lifted his face to it and took his last few breaths as the levels continued to rise. He filled his lungs and pulled his head under.

With only memories of Building Eighteen to guide him, Rhys grabbed the broken door that led to the basement and pulled himself through the hole.

The water level in the building had risen to the same height as in the tunnels. Rhys swam as high as he could. The diseased sank to the bottom so he needed to stay as far away from them as possible. There could be hundreds of the fuckers down below, desperate to drag him under.

When he lifted his head to breathe, his skull cracked against the concrete ceiling. His pulse raced and his head spun. He had no margin for error now. A deep breath and Rhys pushed his head beneath the surface again.

Panic threatened to steal his oxygen and his limbs had turned numb, but if he remained at the top, he'd be okay. The diseased swam like rocks, and with at least two metres of water, they wouldn't be able to get to him... in theory, anyway.

Rhys' hand scraped one of the rough walls. The bobbled surface stung his frozen fingertips, but he kept the wall on his right. It helped him maintain his bearings. If he followed it, it had to lead to the stairs that could get him out of there.

In theory.

The sound of his own pulse continued to pound like a bass drum and a sharp pain tore through his ever-restricting lungs.

WHITE LIGHT EXPLODED THROUGH RHYS' VISION WHEN HE crashed, head first, into a wall. Dizziness rocked his world but he managed to fight against the lure of it as it tried to take his consciousness away.

He felt his way along the wall and found the gap… The stairs! It had to be the stairway out. A combination of brain freeze and the headache from the impact ran sharp needles of pain through Rhys' eyeballs. His sinuses burned.

Rhys swam through the gap into the stairs. His head continued to spin and he lost his bearings. After every strong stroke, he hoped to burst through the surface, but he didn't find it. The pipe had well and truly flooded the place. Either that or he was aimed at the floor.

A glance up and he saw light. *Thank fuck*. His heart accelerated. The last few metres were the worst part so far. The prospect of oxygen wound everything tighter as if he could pop at any moment.

One final push and he strove to get his head above the water.

Then something grabbed his ankle and pulled him back.

Rhys kicked and bubbles burst from his mouth when he shouted. It spent what oxygen he had left in his lungs. A shrill whine sounded in his ears—a requiem for the drowning.

He got pulled farther back.

The light up ahead grew darker.

Rhys kicked out to try and break free again, but whatever had a hold of him pulled him deeper.

CHAPTER 40

W hat had seemed like a reachable light just seconds ago shot away from Rhys as he flew backwards. A vice-like grip wrapped so tightly around his ankle it stung. Any tighter and it would surely break the bones within it. Rhys kicked and shook his foot, but it did nothing to get the thing off him.

With every second that passed, the burn in Rhys' lungs increased. With no chance of air or escape, he let go of his fight and fell limp.

Far from peaceful, but accepting of his fate, Rhys went with the thing that pulled on his leg.

Until something broke the water above him.

Was the diseased above so desperate to get to him, it was prepared to drown?

A tight grip on his collar and the diseased from above yanked hard. It broke him free from the monster's grip below, but his shirt cut into his throat as Rhys rushed toward the surface.

Rhys broke through the water, lay up the stairs, and

inhaled so hard his hungry breath sounded like a donkey's bray.

The breath brought clarity and gave Rhys just enough time to see the dark form of the diseased as it moved in for the kill…

But the bite never came.

Several deep coughs and Rhys vomited all over the concrete stairs. A series of quick and light breaths, his throat half clogged with watery bile, and he vomited again.

The thing that had dragged him free withdrew and pulled him farther up the stairs. Each concrete step sent a sharp crack through his knees as he slipped over one and crashed into the next.

As Rhys coughed, spluttered, and fought for air, stars swam in his vision. He vomited again.

After a few more seconds, the tension that had tightened Rhys' throat eased off and he took a deep and unrestricted breath. When he looked up again, his vision had cleared to the point where he recognised his friend. "Dave?"

Dave stopped and turned to him. He half-smiled and lifted a gentle shrug. "All right, mate?"

"What the fuck happened? Where did you *go*?"

Instead of a reply, Dave grabbed Rhys beneath his arms and lifted him to his feet.

Rhys' legs held, but he shook, coughed several times, and vomited water again.

Dave drove heavy pats against Rhys' back. Each wet slap stung the space between his shoulder blades and his words came out in quick, panicked bursts. "The water was so strong down there it knocked me over. I couldn't find you again. I couldn't see anything. When I found the door, I swam through. What else could I do? I'm *sorry* I left you, man."

Rhys shook his head and half laughed. "Don't worry

about it. You're free. We're both free." When he looked down at the water, he saw the level visibly rise. "I'd hoped it would fill up quickly, but I'm surprised at just how bloody quick. It won't be long before this water's pouring out into the street."

Rhys looked past his friend up the flight of stairs. They led to the next level of the basement. "There's no diseased down here with us?"

A shake of his head and Dave said, "Not that I can see. The stupid fuckers seemed so desperate to get to us, that they didn't know when to retreat to save their own skin. It looks like the water took all of them out. Your plan worked, buddy."

Dizziness rocked Rhys' world when he nodded. "Thank fuck!"

When Dave looked down at the water, Rhys did the same. The pair stood in relative silence. The water lapped, and Rhys breathed heavily. He couldn't hear any of the diseased.

After another step had been claimed by the water level rise, Dave slapped Rhys on the back again. It stung just as bad as before. "Come on, man, let's get the fuck out of here."

A knot of anxiety tied in Rhys' stomach. "I feel naked without a weapon. Did you manage to keep my baseball—?"

Before Rhys could finish, Dave shook his head. "No, we'd best just run fucking fast. We're alive; that's better than we could have hoped for fifteen minutes ago. Oh, and the water seems to have helped my cough."

Cold and exhausted, Rhys shook. He took a deep gulp. "Okay."

CHAPTER 41

The climb up the long flight of stairs that led to the reception area of Building Thirteen aggravated the burn in Rhys' lungs. Water damage and his lack of fitness combined to make every breath less nourishing than the one that had preceded it. If they came across a ravenous horde, he had no fucking chance right now.

Close to the top of the stairs, Rhys stopped, wiped his sodden hair away from his eyes, linked his fingers behind his head, and winced as he pulled shallow breaths into his body.

When Dave gripped the handle of the door that led through to the reception area, Rhys lifted the palm of his hand. Too exhausted for even one word, he needed a minute or two to rest.

Although Dave waited, a tightness gripped his face and his eyes narrowed as he watched Rhys. He ground his teeth and then bit his bottom lip. He tapped an impatient beat against his wet thighs. A glance through the window into the reception area, and he looked back at Rhys again and raised his eyebrows.

A couple more deep breaths and Rhys winced at the pain in his lungs. Every time he inhaled to a certain point, a sharp ache stopped him going any further. It would take more than a few minutes to recover. He'd have to deal with it as best as he could. He tugged on his wet shirt that had stuck to his torso, removed the walkie-talkie from his sodden pocket, and switched it on.

Nothing. *Hardly a fucking surprise.* He laughed ironically. "It would seem that a walkie-talkie's an even worse swimmer than I am."

Dave watched him in silence and his eyebrows pinched in the middle.

Rhys held the walkie-talkie up. "Fucking thing's fucked." He threw it down the concrete stairs. The plastic object clattered against every step on the way down before it landed in the water at the bottom with a pathetic *plop*.

In the absolute silence that followed, Rhys listened for the screams of the diseased in the foyer. Dave stood with his shoulders tense.

After a couple of seconds with no roar, Rhys said, "Didn't think that one through, did I? Sorry, mate."

Dave paused for a second longer and said, "No. It seems like it's okay out there though. Good to find that out, I suppose."

A pat of his other trouser pocket and Rhys' heart stopped for a second. "It's *gone*, Dave."

"What's gone?"

"The bark! The bark that Flynn painted and varnished for me. I've *lost* it." He pointed at the rising water level. "It's down there." The photo remained in Rhys' top pocket, but when he removed it, the water had damaged it so badly the paper had turned to mush.

The world in front of Rhys blurred and his eyeballs stung.

"Oh, fuck." A blink sent a stream of tears down each cheek. "Fuck it! Fuck!"

Rhys looked at his friend. "What the fuck are we going to do, Dave? I've left my kid with a *stranger*. She could have done god knows what to him. Larissa's gone, so even if I do get back to him, I've got to explain that Mummy's dead. We've still got to get across the open space between this tower and the draw bridge without getting attacked, and we have *no* fucking weapons now."

The restriction had never left his chest, but the grief and panic accelerated his pulse and the entire area around his heart wound tighter. Each shallow breath did nothing to satisfy him or settle his furious heartbeat.

Like before, Dave dropped a heavy hand on Rhys' shoulder and stared into his eyes. Calmness sat in his dark irises and sweat glistened on his brow. Rhys continued to shiver from his damp clothes and the cold basement.

"Whatever happens, Rhys, I'm going to make sure we get off this island and back to your boy." He shook Rhys when he repeated, "*Whatever* happens. We need to focus on what's in front of us right now and deal with that. At the moment, all we have is a closed door. We don't know what's on the other side."

"Exactly," Rhys said.

"But that doesn't mean the diseased are there. We don't know, so we shouldn't try to guess. All we can actually do next is open the door, wouldn't you agree?"

Rhys nodded.

Another squeeze of his shoulder and Dave dipped his head to get eye contact with Rhys again. "I know we're going to be okay, man. We've come this far. Just like we don't know what's on the other side of this door, we don't know what's happening with Vicky. All you have is the word of a psychopath, and what's that worth?" Dave lifted Rhys' wrist and looked at the Superman watch. "Come on, man, we only have about twenty minutes left."

Dave pulled the door open and Rhys followed him through.

≈

LIKE THE LAST RECEPTION AREA, THE ONE IN BUILDING Thirteen had been trashed. Too many people had been forced to wait around for too long. Blankets, cups, food wrappers; the place looked a state.

The pair crossed the foyer on high alert as they both looked for signs of the diseased. It seemed quiet. Maybe all of them had drowned themselves down in the basement.

When they got to the front of Building Thirteen—the double doors open to the outside world—Rhys caught the faintest whiff of rot. "This is where I helped Oscar fight the three diseased. Not that he needed my help. The fucker blatantly lured me in because he needed to find someone to get him into the tower. He needed someone to help him turn the order to incinerate off. And he needed someone to watch his back because his leg was fucked. I feel so fucking *stupid* when I think about it now. He reeled me in a treat."

"At least he got you to The Alpha Tower."

Rhys sighed. "Yeah, I suppose he did. I may not have stood a chance without him."

Dave's cough returned. Deep barks ran through him and he bent over double. The enclosed space at the front of Building Thirteen reverberated with the violent expulsions. When he pulled back up again, sweat glistened on his brow.

Rhys' wet clothes and the fading sun made him shiver again. "You okay, man? *How* are you still hot?"

Dave nodded and coughed again. "I guess I haven't recovered from the fire like I thought I had. Once you've been that warm it's hard to cool down."

Before Rhys could say anything else, Dave's eyes widened and he pointed over toward the drawbridge.

Rhys looked over and lost his words for a moment. After he'd opened his mouth once or twice, he finally said, "Larissa?"

CHAPTER 42

"You ready?" Dave said.

The breeze caught Rhys and his skin tightened with gooseflesh. The heat of the day had well and truly gone now. His damp clothes clung to him and he clenched his jaw against the cold. It seemed impossible that Dave still had a sweat-dampened brow. With a final deep breath as he looked across the space between them and Larissa, he dipped a sharp nod. "Yep."

Without another word, Dave set off and Rhys followed him. The run came as a welcome relief. Sure, he ached like before, worse in fact, but the movement helped his frigid muscles unwind and raised his body temperature.

The pair watched their surroundings. It seemed empty; the sounds of slaughter came from the city behind—screams, cries, roars… always the roar of rage from the diseased. It wouldn't be long before it found its way to the bridge.

The florist on Rhys' right looked like it had a few hours previously—abandoned and bloody. The unfinished buildings stood as two large phallic skeletons. Again, abandoned. The food booths had changed. The metal shells had gone and each one had an open door as if the occupant had fled—even the one with the woman he'd spoken to inside. Hopefully she took Rhys' advice and made it out across the river. Hopefully they hadn't taken all the boats when they escaped.

With the sound of his own breath loud inside his skull, Rhys focused on the bridge. He couldn't do anything for the woman in the booth now. If she hadn't run already, she'd have to deal with this world in whatever way she saw fit. Rhys couldn't afford to help her… his little boy needed him.

As they moved towards Larissa, Rhys saw she had her attention on the ground. She sobbed and shook her head. The drawbridge remained raised behind her. Even from about twenty metres away, Rhys saw the evidence that a mob of diseased had come up against it. Blood coated the metal surface from what must have been an onslaught of fists and bodies as if the solid barrier would yield to their ineffectual assault. They must have attacked it for long after he left to help Oscar.

When they got closer to her, Larissa jumped and looked up with wide eyes. Recognition softened her features and her grief returned as it contorted and twisted her face. "Clive's dead," she called out.

Rhys glanced around and pressed his finger across his lips. The place may be free of the diseased now, but that could change in an instant, especially if she shot her mouth off.

Then Rhys saw the body by her feet. Clive, or what remained of Clive, lay lifeless on the concrete. The markings of the diseased streaked his face as dried bloody tears, and his head had been caved in. Larissa didn't have a weapon. Rhys pointed down at Clive and said, "How the fuck did—"

He stopped when he looked down. Blood coated the heel of her right shoe. A look from her shoe to Clive's face and back to her shoe again, and Rhys winced.

"I had to kill him," she said as she shivered and breathed rapidly. The pace of her words quickened and became shriller. "I *had* to kill him. We got away but he'd been bitten. What else could I *do*? I *had* to do it, Rhys. I *had* to kill him."

Even though the woman clearly needed it, hugging her felt like the most unnatural thing in the world. It had been a long time since they'd touched one another.

The kick of her strong perfume made Rhys wrinkle his nose. Anchored firmly in his pain, the strong reek dragged him back to the arguments, the nights he slept on the sofa, and the time he eventually packed his bags and left. Despite a deep desire to let go of her, he held on as she shook in his arms. He did the best he could. "Come on, Larissa, everything's going to be okay. We'll get off this island and everything will be fine. Flynn's waiting for us on the other side."

"But what about *Clive*?" Her voice carried over the open space.

"You need to keep your voice down."

She shouted louder. "*Keep* my fucking voice down? I've just stamped the fuck out of the man I love."

Rhys stepped away from her and clenched his fist. The desire to punch her tightened in his right arm. He wouldn't let her hysteria put Flynn in any more danger—especially when it was over Clive. A shared look with Dave and he relaxed a little. He softened his tone. "If you don't shut up, Flynn will be an orphan. Is that what you want?"

Heavy sobs stuttered through her and she shook her head.

"Look," Rhys said while he pointed toward the river, "there are some boats down there. We need to get to them so we can cross to the other side. Once we're safe you can grieve, but not here. Not now."

When Rhys looked at his watch, Larissa said, "That's Flynn's watch."

"I borrowed it. I had to. We have about fifteen minutes before this place is ablaze. If we're not off the island by then, we ain't ever getting off it, and Flynn will lose his Mummy and Daddy."

Larissa continued to cry. It carried across the open space in front of the city.

Before Rhys could berate her again, the roar of the diseased answered her call.

"Fucking hell, Larissa. This is why you need to keep your fucking voice down." With a hard grip clamped on her upper arm, Rhys dragged her away from the dead Clive. "*Come on*, we need to go before you get us all killed."

At first, she resisted, but when Rhys tugged harder, she came with him.

When the three of them made it to the top of the riverbank, Rhys scanned the area. Several rowboats remained and bobbed in the water. Footprints ran from the top of the riverbank down to the shoreline. Maybe the woman in the food pod had gotten away. When he looked across, he saw boats on the other side. Although muddy, the riverbank looked no harder to travel down this side than it had on the other. At least the boats were already in the water. A look behind and his blood ran cold. "Fuck!"

Both Larissa and Dave also looked behind.

A rush of diseased flew from several alleyways. They

came out in a continuous stream as if the entire city had answered Larissa's call. A quick glance at Dave and Rhys saw his friend's eyes widen. Dave looked back at him, dipped a nod, and they both ran. They dragged the grieving Larissa with them.

CHAPTER 43

The soggier ground closer to the boats pulled at Rhys' feet. Every step tugged harder than the last. The roar of the diseased screamed louder than before. Any second now and the ones at the front would crest the brow of the hill.

Larissa stopped and grabbed Rhys' arm. It snapped him to a halt.

"I've lost my shoe, Rhys."

Rhys breathed heavily and his pulse thudded. "*What*?"

She pointed at the ground behind her. "I've lost my shoe."

The first batch of diseased appeared at the top of the hill. Clumsy as always, they looked like they'd fall as they began their descent down the riverbank.

Rhys froze in the intensity of their collective projection of hate. "Fuck your shoe," he said, "we're going to die if we don't fucking move." A tug on Larissa's arm and they ran again.

The ground squelched louder than ever but they made it to a rowboat before the diseased caught up. Dave stood back while Rhys held the boat for Larissa to climb in. The urge to kick her up the arse ran through him. "Do you want to take any more fucking time, love?"

Although Larissa replied, Rhys didn't listen as he pulled himself in after her. The vessel rocked in the water, but when he flopped into it, it stabilised quickly.

Dave pushed them farther into the water. Rhys watched his friend. He sweated now more than ever. The effort from the run had clearly taken it out of him. Or was it more than that? He continued to watch his friend and dread sank in his gut. An ache the size of a golf ball swelled in his throat.

When they were so far out Dave had to tread water, he grabbed the edge of the boat as if to climb in.

Rhys restrained him with a hand against his clammy forehead. He'd ignored his gut too many times and he couldn't do it again. Not now. Not with them so close. Flynn needed his parents.

Wide eyes stared back at him. Then Dave dropped his head.

Grief rushed through Rhys in a hot wave. *Of all the times to be right...* Tears stung Rhys' eyes and his mouth buckled.

On the riverbank, a wall of diseased rushed toward the water. Their arms windmilled as they fought for balance. They whacked one another frequently, but none seemed to notice.

Rhys tried to clear the lump in his throat. It wouldn't budge and his voice shook as he said, "When did it happen?"

Dave wiped his sweating brow as he trod water. He then pushed back toward the riverbank. The gap between the friends widened as Larissa rowed them away.

Dave swam backwards and raised his pelvis to the sky. He pulled his top up and showed Rhys the dark wound on his stomach. "It was when I was swimming out of the tunnels.

One of them got me. I'd hoped the water would have kept it clean, and that maybe I wouldn't turn."

Heat surged through Rhys' entire body. "Why the fuck wouldn't you turn? You've been *bitten*, you fucking idiot. Why wouldn't you fucking turn?" Rhys started to cry and slumped down on the bench in the boat. "Why did you let them bite you, man? Why didn't you take more fucking care?"

Grief twisted Dave's features. Then a twitch ran through him—a snapshot of fury. "It seems to have delayed it somewhat. At least I helped you get off the island, eh?" Another twitch of the disease tore through him.

A tightness gripped Dave's features as he looked from one of Rhys' eyes to the other. "I'm scared, Rhys. I don't want to become one of them." He twitched again.

After several stuttered breaths, Rhys finally managed to force his words past his despair. The distance between them had grown to the point where he needed to shout. "I know, man. I know you don't. I'm *so* sorry. I didn't mean to get angry with you."

A forced smile and Dave pointed at Rhys. "Just make sure you get to Flynn, yeah? Go be with your boy." Another sharp twitch snapped through him that sent one of his arms away from his body.

Choked by his grief, Rhys watched his friend head back to shore.

When he got to shallow water, Dave stood up, and without another word, turned around to face the oncoming mob. The frequency of the twitches increased and turned his movements jerky. The diseased continued to rush over the hill. The ones at the front had nearly caught up to Dave.

When they did, every single one of them ignored him.

They ran around him and splashed into the water after Rhys and Larissa.

"They're leaving him alone," Rhys said. "They *know* he's one of them."

Although Larissa didn't reply, he felt her hand on his back. Rhys watched his best friend succumb to the virus and his vision blurred with his tears.

Dave grabbed the diseased as they passed him and he tossed them to the ground. But for every one he knocked over, ten more made it through.

The monsters splashed into the water, and like before, each and every one of them disappeared beneath the surface. Dave continued to fight.

"We don't need Dave to protect us now," Rhys said as he watched his friend's ineffective battle. "We need him later. We need him on this fucking boat with us. We need him without a huge fucking bite on his fucking stomach. We need…" He couldn't get the words past his tears.

Rhys felt the gentle touch of Larissa's hand on his back again.

CHAPTER 44

As they crossed the river, Rhys stared at his lap and his tears fell down between his legs. He continued to look down and drew a deep breath before he said, "When I was in the city, I found something out about the woman who has Flynn."

Larissa stopped rowing.

Tense in anticipation of the response, Rhys continued anyway. "She's not who I thought she was."

"Who is she?"

"I don't know."

Larissa's voice became more high-pitched. "What do you mean, you don't know? She has our boy, Rhys."

Rhys' heart thudded when he looked up at her. He knew she'd behave like this, although, to be fair, he'd react in exactly the same way. "You think I don't fucking know that? Someone helped me get to The Alpha Tower. His name was Oscar. At least that's what he told me it was. A lot later on, I found out he was a terrorist from The East. He knew her."

"And you've *left* Flynn with her? What the fuck?"

"*Obviously* I didn't know any of this at the time."

"So what does she have to do with The East?"

"I don't know."

"You've got to give me something more, Rhys."

"I *don't* know. He knew her name, that's all I know. I may have said it during the time we spent together. Maybe he's using the fact that I forgot to mention it against me, but I don't know. We just need to get to the other side. Hopefully everything's okay."

"Hopefully?"

Rhys ground his jaw and stared at the woman he used to love. He didn't speak again.

When the boat bumped into the bank on the other side, Rhys looked back across the river. Through all of the diseased —the hatred, the snarling, the growls, the roars—he saw Dave. Just like all of the others, he stared pure malice at Rhys. His best friend. Rhys' view blurred again and his throat burned.

With barely any strength left in his exhausted body, Rhys stood up on shaky legs. He turned his back on his friend and got out of the boat.

The ground pulled at his feet again. A thick bog for the first few metres near the riverbank, it threatened to take what little energy Rhys had left in him. Nevertheless, he pushed on and dragged the boat behind him.

When its base had dug into the ground, he held his hand out for Larissa to help her hop onto the shore.

She jumped down and stared at him.

Rhys turned his back on her and walked off up the hill.

CHAPTER 45

Were it not for the fact that Flynn would be waiting for him, Rhys wouldn't have made it to the top of the riverbank. Exhausted both emotionally and physically, he felt just about ready to throw the fucking towel in.

When he got to the top and saw the police car, he forgot his aches and pains. He broke into a run. Clumsy with tiredness, he crashed into the car, the metal hot from the day.

After he'd pulled the driver's door open, what small amount of strength he had in his body abandoned him.

When Larissa arrived at his side, she shrieked. "What's *happened*, Rhys? Where's our boy? What's happened to him?"

Although Rhys opened and closed his mouth, he couldn't get the words out. Blood coated the interior of the car. It soaked the seats to the point where it pooled on them. It had turned the wheel and dashboard slick, and dripped off the indicator stalks. The metallic reek made Rhys' stomach turn.

Before Rhys could speak, static hissed from the radio in the car. When he leaned in, blood pushed up from the seat and spread between his fingers. He grabbed the radio mic. "Hello."

Out of breath and panicked, Vicky said, "Rhys, it's me. I've fucked up big time, but you can trust me. Please believe me when I say that."

Rhys gripped the mic so hard it hurt his hand. He shouted, "Where's Flynn?"

"With me. He's okay."

"Where are you?"

"I had to move."

"Where are you?"

Another voice came over the radio. It sounded farther away from Vicky. The man who spoke was clearly chasing her. "Come back here, you bitch."

Then he heard Flynn's voice. "I'm scared. Where are we going? I want my mum and dad. Why are we running?"

"Vicky," Rhys said as his spittle sprayed the microphone, "where are you? What's happening?"

A clattering sound and the radio went dead.

"Vicky?"

Nothing.

Rhys banged the mic against the car's dashboard. "Fuck! Fuck, fuck, fuck, fuck, fuck!"

When he stood up, he wiped the blood from his hands onto his trousers. A deep *whoosh* then sounded out behind him. When he turned around, he saw flames in Summit City jump from the ground. They leaped about five metres into the air and rushed through the streets like a flood.

The blast of heat blew Rhys' hair back. It rocked him on his heels.

Numb and exhausted, Rhys stood and stared at the burning city. He looked at Larissa. "How the fuck are we supposed to just wait here? How long will she be? When do we accept that she ain't coming back?"

Larissa didn't respond. Instead, she stared at the burning city through unblinking and glazed eyes.

Rhys looked into the car again. He'd been too shocked to notice it the first time around, but now he couldn't see anything else. "Fuck," he said.

"What?" Larissa asked.

Rhys pointed at the axe on the back seat. "That's Oscar's axe."

Ends.

~

Thank you for reading The Alpha Plague 2. If you'd like to read the next book in the series:

The Alpha Plague 3 is available now at www.michaelrobertson.co.uk

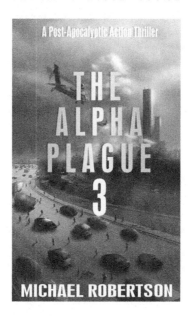

Support the Author

Dear reader, as an independent author I don't have the resources of a huge publisher. If you like my work and would like to see more from me in the future, there are two things you can do to help: leaving a review, and a word-of-mouth referral.

Releasing a book takes many hours and hundreds of dollars. I love to write, and would love to continue to do so. All I ask is that you leave a review. It shows other readers that you've enjoyed the book and will encourage them to give it a try too. The review can be just one sentence, or as long as you like.

ABOUT THE AUTHOR

Like most children born in the seventies, Michael grew up with Star Wars in his life. An obsessive watcher of the films, and an avid reader from an early age, he found himself taken over with stories whenever he let his mind wander.

Those stories had to come out.

He hopes you enjoy reading his books as much as he does writing them.

Michael loves to travel when he can. He has a young family, who are his world, and when he's not reading, he enjoys walking so he can dream up more stories.

Contact
www.michaelrobertson.co.uk
subscribers@michaelrobertson.co.uk

ALSO BY MICHAEL ROBERTSON

THE SHADOW ORDER:

The Shadow Order

The First Mission - Book Two of The Shadow Order

The Crimson War - Book Three of The Shadow Order

Eradication - Book Four of The Shadow Order

Fugitive - Book Five of The Shadow Order

Enigma - Book Six of The Shadow Order

Prophecy - Book Seven of The Shadow Order

The Faradis - Book Eight of The Shadow Order

The Complete Shadow Order Box Set - Books 1 - 8

∽

NEON HORIZON:

The Blind Spot - A Science Fiction Thriller - Neon Horizon
Book One.

Prime City - A Science Fiction Thriller - Neon Horizon Book Two.

Bounty Hunter - A Science Fiction Thriller - Neon Horizon Book
Three.

Connection - A Science Fiction Thriller - Neon Horizon Book Four.

Reunion - A Science Fiction Thriller - Neon Horizon Book Five.

Eight Ways to Kill a Rat - A Science Fiction Thriller - Neon
Horizon Book Six.

Neon Horizon - Books 1 - 3 Box Set - A Science Fiction Thriller.

~

THE ALPHA PLAGUE:

The Alpha Plague: A Post-Apocalyptic Action Thriller

The Alpha Plague 2

The Alpha Plague 3

The Alpha Plague 4

The Alpha Plague 5

The Alpha Plague 6

The Alpha Plague 7

The Alpha Plague 8

The Complete Alpha Plague Box Set - Books 1 - 8

BEYOND THESE WALLS:

Protectors - Book one of Beyond These Walls

National Service - Book two of Beyond These Walls

Retribution - Book three of Beyond These Walls

Collapse - Book four of Beyond These Walls

After Edin - Book five of Beyond These Walls

Three Days - Book six of Beyond These Walls

The Asylum - Book seven of Beyond These Walls

Between Fury and Fear - Book eight of Beyond These Walls

Before the Dawn - Book nine of Beyond These Walls

The Wall - Book ten of Beyond These Walls

Divided - Book eleven of Beyond These Walls

Escape - Book twelve of Beyond These Walls

Beyond These Walls - Books 1 - 6 Box Set

Beyond These Walls - Books 7 - 9 Box Set

~

TALES FROM BEYOND THESE WALLS:

Fury - Book one of Tales From Beyond These Walls

~

OFF-KILTER TALES:

The Girl in the Woods - A Ghost's Story - Off-Kilter Tales
Book One

Rat Run - A Post-Apocalyptic Tale - Off-Kilter Tales Book Two

~

Masked - A Psychological Horror

CRASH:

Crash - A Dark Post-Apocalyptic Tale

Crash II: Highrise Hell

Crash III: There's No Place Like Home

Crash IV: Run Free

Crash V: The Final Showdown

~

NEW REALITY:

New Reality: Truth

New Reality 2: Justice

New Reality 3: Fear

Audiobooks:

CLICK HERE TO VIEW MY FULL AUDIOBOOK LIBRARY.